MARY ANNE AND THE
PLAYGROUND FIGHT

Other books by
Ann M. Martin

P.S. Longer Letter Later
(written with Paula Danziger)
Leo the Magnificat
Rachel Parker, Kindergarten Show-off
Eleven Kids, One Summer
Ma and Pa Dracula
Yours Turly, Shirley
Ten Kids, No Pets
Slam Book
Just a Summer Romance
Missing Since Monday
With You and Without You
Me and Katie (the Pest)
Stage Fright
Inside Out
Bummer Summer

THE KIDS IN MS. COLMAN'S CLASS series
BABY-SITTERS LITTLE SISTER series
THE BABY-SITTERS CLUB mysteries
THE BABY-SITTERS CLUB series
CALIFORNIA DIARIES series

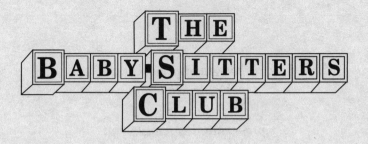

MARY ANNE AND THE PLAYGROUND FIGHT

Ann M. Martin

AN
APPLE
PAPERBACK

SCHOLASTIC INC.
New York Toronto London Auckland Sydney

The author gratefully acknowledges
Diane Molleson
for her help in
preparing this manuscript.

Cover art by Hodges Soileau

ISBN 0-590-05998-X

12 11 10 9 8 7 6 5 4 3 2 1   8 9/9 0 1 2 3/0

Printed in the U.S.A.   40

First Scholastic printing, June 1998

CHAPTER 1

"On the final," Ms. Belcher was saying, "I would like you to be able to define some of the major poetic forms such as the sonnet and the villanelle."

"Who's the villain?" shouted Alan Gray.

Ms. Belcher and the rest of my English class ignored Alan. That's sometimes the best way to deal with him. He's our class pest, who thinks everything he says is hilarious, even though it's usually not.

"I also expect you to give me examples of alliteration and assonance," Ms. Belcher continued.

I flipped through my notes. A sonnet, I had written, is a fourteen-line poem with a certain rhyme scheme.

By now, Ms. Belcher was talking about something called onomatopoeia. But I was still thinking about the sonnet. An example of a sonnet is Shakespeare's poem that begins,

"Shall I compare thee to a summer's day?"

I sighed and looked out the window. I could not wait for summer. I usually love English, and reading and writing, and anything to do with books. But today I was having trouble concentrating.

Outside a robin perched on the windowsill. Oak trees rustled in the breeze and puffy white clouds floated across the sky. The grass looked lush and green and welcoming. What was I doing inside? All I wanted to do was sit on that grass and talk to my friends about what we were going to do this summer.

I always look forward to summer because that's when Dawn Schafer, my stepsister, comes back to Stoneybrook to visit. Dawn is one of my two best friends, and I miss her more than I can say. I cried my eyes out when she decided to move back to California. But I'm getting ahead of my story. I'll tell you more about my family later. First let me introduce myself.

I'm Mary Anne Spier. I'm thirteen years old. I'm pretty short, and I have brown hair and brown eyes. People say I'm very sensitive, which is true. It doesn't take much for me to start crying. When my boyfriend, Logan, and I go to the movies, Logan often brings a box of tissues because I cry so much. (Is that embarrassing or what?) I'm shy too, but sometimes I think that being sensitive and shy helps me listen to people.

I live in Stoneybrook, Connecticut, where I'm in the eighth grade at Stoneybrook Middle School. My other best friend, Kristy Thomas, is in the eighth grade too. Kristy is as outgoing and assertive as I am shy. I guess opposites attract because we've been best friends for as long as I can remember.

I've lived in Stoneybrook my whole life. I'm an only child, and my mother died when I was a baby. I don't remember her at all, but people who knew her are always telling me I look and act like her. For example, like me, my mother liked to sew and hated to cook.

When my mother died, my dad was devastated, as you can imagine. He even sent me to live with my grandparents in Nebraska until he could cope a little better. I was too little to remember Nebraska now, but I do know that for most of my life my dad was rather strict with me. Kristy used to call him the King of Rules. Until eighth grade, I had to go to bed earlier than all my friends. And Dad used to pick out my clothes, which meant I wore babyish frilly blouses and long little-girlish skirts. I was not allowed to have my ears pierced, and I had to wear my hair in braids or pigtails. (Ugh.)

It took Dad forever to accept that I was

3

growing up. Fortunately, with the help of my friends, I was able to encourage him to relax a little. Now I can pick out my own clothes, within reason. I like simple, conservative things — no frills or lace ever again (except maybe when I get married). I also have pierced ears and a haircut I like. I even have a reasonable curfew. So you see, things have changed for the better since I've been in eighth grade.

Dad is a lot happier too. Lately there's been a big change in our life — Sharon. Sharon happens to be Dawn's mom . . . and my dad's new wife.

Dad and Sharon were high school sweethearts, right here in Stoneybrook. They broke up, though, because Sharon's parents did not approve of my dad. (Hmmph.) Sharon moved to California and lost touch with my father. Many years later, when I was in seventh grade, I became good friends with a girl named Dawn Schafer, who had just moved to Stoneybrook from California with her divorced mother and younger brother, Jeff. (Do you see a family picture emerging?)

It took Dawn and me awhile to realize that Dawn's mom was *the* Sharon in Dad's past, but when we made that connection, nothing could stop us. We reintroduced them, and Dad and Sharon fell in love all over again.

This is further proof that opposites attract, as

I said before. Dad and Sharon could not be more different. My dad, Mr. Neat and Organized, is a lawyer. He alphabetizes the spices in our kitchen cabinet. He arranges his socks by color. And he always reads the newspaper in the same order — the business section first, then international news, national news, and (finally) local news.

Sharon, on the other hand, never puts anything in its place. I often find her sunglasses in the refrigerator and her mail in the bathroom. Plus, Sharon, like Dawn and Jeff, likes to eat healthy foods. And *no* red meat.

But all this does not really matter because Dad and Sharon love each other and are very happy. And so am I, because now I have a great stepsister and stepbrother, a great stepmom, and a great place to live. Dad and I moved into Sharon's cool farmhouse on Burnt Hill Road. It was built in the 1700s, and it has low ceilings, narrow hallways, a brick fireplace, a barn in the back, and best of all, a secret passageway that may be haunted.

Unfortunately, Dawn does not live in our farmhouse anymore, at least not full-time. As I mentioned, she moved back to California to live with her dad (Jeff had done the same thing earlier). It wasn't that they didn't get along with my dad and me, or that they hated Stoneybrook. They were just terribly homesick.

And soon Dawn was going to be back in Stoneybrook for the first time since Christmas. Usually she visits more often, but she's been going through a lot in California. For one thing, Dawn's father remarried too. His new wife is named Carol. As if that weren't enough excitement, Dawn's father and Carol just had a baby, a beautiful little girl named Elizabeth Grace — Gracie, for short. (Dawn sent me pictures.)

I can't wait to hear more about how Dawn is doing with the baby. At least she's had a lot of practice baby-sitting. We both have. Dawn and I are members of the Baby-sitters Club, also known as the BSC.

Staring out the window, I sighed. Thinking about Dawn made me miss her more than ever.

Alan Gray (who else?) startled me out of my daydream. He was taking the cartridge out of his ballpoint pen and stuffing the empty tube with a wad of paper. I knew what was coming. He was going to send a spitball flying. He already had the pen in his mouth (how disgusting) and he was aiming at Barbara Hirsch. I wanted to warn her, but I was sitting too far away for her to hear me. (Unless I screamed, which would probably get me into more trouble than Alan.)

I could not believe what happened next. Barbara miraculously leaned over to whisper something to Gordon Brown. The spitball whizzed past her head, just missing her. It landed on Ms. Belcher's arm.

I gulped. Most of the other kids in the class froze and stared straight ahead as Ms. Belcher made a face (who could blame her?) and brushed away the spitball with her hand.

The class was so quiet you could have heard a mouse in the back of the room. Actually, some kids in the back were trying very hard not to laugh. Other kids looked too surprised to say anything. Alan was the only one not looking at our teacher. He stared at the floor, probably wishing he could disappear.

"Alan," Ms. Belcher said firmly as she walked toward him. "You're going to the principal's office right now!" Ms. Belcher is usually pretty mild-mannered, but at that moment she looked as if she wanted to yank Alan's hair out of his head. (I'm exaggerating, but she looked angrier than I'd ever seen her.)

Just then the final bell rang. Everyone in the class, except for Alan, gathered up their books and rushed out of the room.

In the hall, we started spluttering and laughing. "I can't believe it — a direct hit!" Gordon exclaimed.

"I'd believe almost anything when it comes to Alan," Barbara said. Some kids hung around outside the classroom, waiting for Alan and

Ms. Belcher to come out. Not me, though. I walked with Barbara, Gordon, and a few other kids to our lockers.

"I wonder if he'll get suspended for this," Gordon said.

"I wish," said Barbara.

"He'd have to do something a lot more serious than that to get suspended," said a familiar voice. A voice with a slight southern drawl.

"Logan, you heard what happened already?" I asked.

Logan Bruno is my boyfriend. He's handsome and athletic, and he has a southern accent because he's originally from Kentucky.

"News like this travels fast," said Logan, laughing. "Peter filled me in." (Peter Hayes is in my English class and is also on the track team with Logan. They're good friends.)

"What do you think will happen to him?" asked Howie Johnson. By now we had reached our lockers. I pulled out my math and science books. I still had a lot of studying to do for those two finals, which were both on Friday.

"I don't know," said Logan. "He'll probably have a lot of very long detentions."

Alan's big punishment, we soon heard from Melissa Banks, was that he had to stay after school all week and write a thousand-word essay titled "How to Behave." He also had to do some community service for the school, such as

8

help the janitor, Mr. Halprin, take out the trash. (I felt sorry for anyone Alan helped.)

Since it was such a beautiful day, Logan and I decided to walk to the lighthouse after school and maybe do some studying there before our BSC meeting. (Logan is in the Baby-sitters Club too.) I also wanted to daydream again about summer vacation, which would begin in less than a week, when school was over. I couldn't wait.

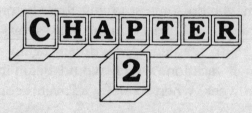

CHAPTER 2

I think Stoneybrook has one of the prettiest lighthouses I've ever seen. Logan thinks it looks like a giant barber pole because it's painted in red and white stripes. The lighthouse is on the edge of town, not far from school on the Long Island Sound. I love sitting at the picnic tables by the lighthouse, breathing in the salty air and watching the waves lap against the rocks, while seagulls fly overhead.

I sighed and opened my math book.

"Don't worry. Soon we can come here and not have any schoolwork to think about," said Logan. He can always read my mind. He sat across from me with his American history book open to the chapter on the Revolutionary War.

"Oh, Mary Anne, Mary Anne. Yooo-hooo, Mary Anne."

I looked up, startled, but I recognized the familiar English accent. It belonged to Miss Rutherford, Victoria Kent's nanny. (We often baby-sit for Victoria, who's eight. Her parents, who are British and distantly related to the royal family, wanted Victoria exposed to Americans during the time they were living in Stoneybrook. That's why they called the BSC when they first saw our flier.) Victoria was running to me now, arms outstretched.

"Hey, Mary Anne!" she shouted. "Isn't this quite the coolest lighthouse?"

I chuckled. Victoria would never have talked that way a few months ago. I could see Miss Rutherford flinching.

"Victoria, there is no need to yell. Mary Anne is not far away."

"So cool," Victoria repeated more softly. Logan and I hid our grins. I stood up to be enveloped in Victoria's big hug.

Today, Victoria was dressed in a T-shirt, jeans, and high-top red sneakers, not exactly the Laura Ashley pinafores and starched white blouses she usually wore.

"Nice outfit," I remarked. But, I admit, I was surprised.

"Isn't it?" said Victoria, seating herself at our table. "Mother and Father let me pick out some really awesome American clothes as a souvenir of my time in the States. You know, we're going back to England at the end of the month."

I nodded. Victoria's parents work for the United Nations. They had only expected to stay in the U.S. for six months, but their assignments had lasted longer than they thought.

"And you know what else?" Victoria continued, scuffing her sneaker in the dirt.

"What?" I asked. I could not believe how American she sounded.

"I don't want to go back to England. I like it here. And what's more, I'm fully Americanized. All the kids on my street say so." This time Logan and I could no longer hide our smiles.

"Victoria, what are you saying?" said Miss Rutherford. "Now, sit here quietly and have your tea without disturbing Mary Anne and Logan." (Tea, as I have learned from Miss Rutherford, is a snack the British have around four o'clock in the afternoon.)

Miss Rutherford reached into her large bag and pulled out a thermos, strawberries, and some little gingerbread cakes.

"Please have some," Miss Rutherford offered, passing the cakes to Logan and me. "Isn't this splendid, Victoria? Now we can have a real tea party."

Victoria put her hands on her hips. "It's not a tea party. It's really more like an after-school snack, isn't it? And I wish we could have Yodels and potato chips, like my classmates."

I bit into the lightest, most delicious gingerbread I've ever tasted. "This food is better," I couldn't help saying.

"Victoria, would you like some apple juice?" asked Miss Rutherford.

"You know, I like it better when you call me Vicki. It sounds more American. Doesn't it, Mary Anne?"

I shrugged. My mouth was full. "It doesn't really make a difference," I said after swallowing.

"Now, Victoria," said Miss Rutherford, "you know your parents prefer your Christian name."

"I don't care what they prefer. It sucks to be moving back to England, now that I like it here so much."

"Don't say *sucks*, Victoria," Miss Rutherford chided.

"Vicki, remember how much you missed England when you first moved here? And you know how much Jezra, Annabelle, and Christina are looking forward to seeing you again," I said. (I had heard a lot about Victoria's best friends in England.)

"Maybe they could visit me here. I know they would just love America."

Miss Rutherford looked at me and sighed.

I decided I'd better talk to my friends in the BSC about Victoria at the meeting. Which reminded me, it was almost time to leave. Kristy, our president, hates when anyone is late. She's almost as bad as my dad that way.

"This meeting of the Baby-sitters Club will come to order," Kristy said twenty minutes later, while looking at the clock. It was five-thirty *sharp*. She sat in a director's chair, the same chair she commandeered at every meeting, and looked at us from under the visor of her baseball cap, the same cap she wore to every meeting.

The Baby-sitters Club meets every Monday, Wednesday, and Friday afternoon from five-thirty to six in Claudia Kishi's room. And why is Claudia's room our official headquarters? For two good reasons. One, Claudia has her own private phone line so clients can call us during meetings (our business hours) to request sitting jobs. And two, Claudia always keeps a generous supply of munchies on hand in case we're hungry, which we always are. At this very moment, Abby Stevenson, Jessica Ramsey, and Mallory Pike were on the rug by Claudia's bed, gorging on potato chips. Kristy was holding a chocolate Ring-Ding in one hand. I was swallowing a fistful of M&M's. And Stacey McGill, who is not allowed to eat sugary food, was munching on a carrot stick.

"Let's take care of dues first," Kristy said.

We groaned. We pay dues every Monday, and we always groan about it. We use the money for club expenses, which include our snacks, gas money for Kristy's brother Charlie who drives her and Abby to the meetings, and items for the Kid-Kits.

Kid-Kits are special boxes filled with games, puzzles, books, crayons, glitter pens, and whatever else we think would be fun for our baby-sitting charges. We don't bring the kits to every job, but they do come in handy when we have new clients, or when we think a job is going to be challenging (because a kid is sick or has to stay indoors because of the weather, for example). The Kid-Kits were Kristy's brainstorm. Which makes sense. She's the one who came up with the idea for the Baby-sitters Club in the first place.

Kristy thought up the BSC one night while listening to her mother make phone call after phone call trying to find a sitter for Kristy's little brother, David Michael. Kristy thought, *What if a person could call one number and reach several sitters at once?*

For Kristy, having an idea is the same as acting on it. In no time at all, she had rounded up three friends: me, Claudia, and Stacey. The Baby-sitters Club was launched . . . and the rest is history, in Stoneybrook, at least.

It's hard to believe there were once only four

people in the BSC. Since then, we have more than doubled in size. Now we have seven full-time members, two associate members to handle overflow business, and one long-distance, honorary member in California — Dawn. We don't need to hand out fliers or put up signs around town anymore. We have more than enough business from satisfied clients and from people to whom we've been recommended.

In order to keep things organized, we have a record book. That's where I come in. I am the club secretary. I keep track of all our schedules and all our jobs, as well as important information about each charge (such as allergies and other medical conditions).

We also have a BSC notebook in which we write about our jobs. A lot of members think the notebook is a big pain because it's like homework, but I really enjoy writing in it. The notebook helps keep us up-to-date on what's happening with our baby-sitting charges. Also, we can look at past entries to help us solve baby-sitting problems. Chances are, whatever the situation, one of us has seen it before and has written it up in the notebook.

The BSC is successful because we're organized, reliable, and have good ideas (such as the notebook and Kid-Kits), and because the members are very different from one another, yet work well together.

To begin, there's Kristy, our super-organized and daring president. These are excellent qualities for running the BSC, I think. They also come in handy in Kristy's large, noisy family. Like me, Kristy is part of a blended family. Hers, however, is a much bigger one than mine. You would not believe all the people who live in Kristy's house: one mother, one stepfather, one grandmother, two older brothers, one younger brother, one adopted younger sister, and (when they're not living alternate months with their mother) one younger stepsister and one younger stepbrother, plus assorted pets.

Luckily, Kristy lives in a mansion, so there's plenty of room for everyone. (Her stepfather, Watson Brewer, is a millionaire as well as a really great guy.)

Claudia, our vice-president, graciously hosts all the meetings. She was under her bed at the moment, frantically searching for her wallet.

"I know I left it in my backpack," she said, her voice muffled. Claudia emerged from under her bed with her handmade red wallet in one hand and a bag of potato chips in the other.

One thing you should know about Claudia is

17

that she has an incredible talent for art and an incredible appetite for junk food. Claudia can sculpt, paint, sew, draw, and make gorgeous jewelry. She also puts together the most striking outfits I've ever seen. On this day she was wearing an oversized black jumpsuit over a white T-shirt with the sleeves rolled up, plus white socks and black high-top sneakers with silver laces. The laces matched her silver nail polish, silver earrings, and the rings she wore on every finger, even her thumb.

"Just in case we run out of food," Claudia was saying, "here's an extra bag of chips — sour cream and onion, my favorite."

The rest of us laughed. No one in Claudia's room was ever likely to go hungry. Claudia manages to stash away more bags of chocolate candy, chips, cupcakes, and soda than the local grocery store. To look at Claudia, you would never think she's a junk food addict. She's very thin, with a creamy complexion, dark brown eyes, and jet-black hair. Claudia also loves Nancy Drew mysteries, which she also keeps hidden since her parents equate Nancy Drew with junk food. Both are forbidden in the Kishi household.

Claudia's sister, Janine, is a certified genius with a high IQ score to prove it. But Claudia, who excels in art, doesn't like school and had to go back to seventh grade for awhile. Luckily, she did well enough to return to eighth grade — our lunch table wasn't the same without her.

Our club treasurer, Stacey, is Claudia's best friend. They share a love of clothes and fashion, though Stacey tends to wear more urban, store-bought clothes than Claudia. Stacey honed her fashion sense in New York City, where she was born and raised.

Unlike Claudia, Stacey cannot eat most junk food. That's because she has diabetes, which means her body can't process refined sugar. So Stacey has to watch what she eats very, very carefully and even give herself insulin injections to make sure she doesn't get sick.

Stacey handles her diabetes with the same assurance and efficiency with which she handles everything else. Maybe that's why she seems older than the other members of the BSC. Also because she's gorgeous and always well dressed. What's more, Stacey is a math whiz. She recently joined the math team at school and became the state champ.

Stacey's parents are divorced. They split up after Stacey's father was transferred back to New York City, so Stacey visits her dad there often.

Abby, our alternate officer, is the newest member of the BSC. She took Dawn's place when she moved to California. And just in time, because we were *swamped* with business.

Abby (short for Abigail) moved to Stoney-brook from Long Island with her mother and her twin sister, Anna. (Abby's father died in a car accident when she was only nine.)

Abby and her twin could not be more different. Like Kristy, Abby is outgoing, energetic, and, lest I forget, extremely athletic. I think soccer is her favorite sport, but she also plays softball, basketball, and volleyball. Last summer, she was on a Unified Special Olympics Team.

You won't find Anna on a sports field. Anna is more like me — quiet, thoughtful, and unathletic. I was hoping she would join the BSC too. We invited her, but she said she didn't have the time. She practices the violin several hours a day and hopes to becomes a professional musician. Anna wears her dark brown hair shorter than Abby's and with bangs, while Abby's hair cascades in long ringlets around her face.

One more thing I should tell you about Abby is that she has asthma and is allergic to almost everything — dust, dogs (but not cats), tomatoes, shellfish, milk, cheese, and pollen. Her backpack is filled with tissues, antihistamines, inhalers, and her asthma medicine, but she doesn't let her asthma get her down. Luckily, it doesn't interfere with her sports.

Jessi and Mallory are junior members of the BSC because they're in sixth grade and can't baby-sit at night unless it's for their families. Each is the oldest kid in her family and is enlisted to do a lot of baby-sitting for her siblings. This makes them great members, since they have so much sitting practice.

Mallory, who has seven siblings, including a set of triplets, has reddish-brown hair, pale skin with freckles, and — to her despair — wears glasses and braces. (I think she looks great in glasses, but she wants contacts as soon as possible. And she can't wait to lose the braces.)

Mallory and Jessi are best friends, and they have a lot in common. They share a passion for horses and horse stories, especially books by Marguerite Henry. Both of them know exactly what they want to do when they grow up. Mallory wants to be a writer; her stories have already won prizes in school. And Jessi, our ballerina, gets up at 5:29 every morning to practice at the *barre* her parents set up for her in their basement. She also studies ballet at a school in Stamford, the biggest city near Stoneybrook.

Jessi moved to Stoneybrook from New Jersey with her mother, father, younger sister, and baby brother. (Her aunt now lives with the family too.)

Jessi already looks and acts like a ballet dancer. She is one of the most graceful people I have ever met, and she often wears her hair in a dancer's bun at the nape of her neck. She also loves to dress in leotards, which she wears with pants, skirts, and under sweaters and jackets. Jessi is perfect dancer height, has brown skin, dark brown hair, and huge brown eyes.

Our associate members are Logan Bruno (my boyfriend) and Shannon Kilbourne. Associate members don't have to attend meetings, but both happened to be at that day's meeting, which is unusual. Logan always seems to have track or softball practice. And Shannon? Well, Shannon is a member of the French Club, the Astronomy Club, the Honor Society, the debate team, and she acts in school plays, when her schedule permits. (Isn't it a good thing associate members don't have to attend meetings?)

Shannon is the only member of the BSC who doesn't go to Stoneybrook Middle School. She attends a private school, Stoneybrook Day School, with her two sisters. When Shannon is not in her school uniform, she likes to wear preppy, kind of casual clothes. And she loves red, which looks great with her thick, curly blonde hair.

By now, Stacey had collected dues and Claudia had fielded three baby-sitting phone calls.

"Any other business?" Kristy asked.

This was the time for me to speak up.

"There's a problem with Victoria Kent," I said.

"There is?" Claudia held her Yodel in midair. In fact, as soon as I said Victoria's name everyone stopped eating and stared at me. Everyone in the club likes Victoria. Mallory finds her "fascinating" and is writing a story about her called "The Real Princess."

"Well, as you know, she's moving back to England at the end of the month, but she doesn't want to. She feels Stoneybrook is home now."

"And she's acting more American than most Americans," Logan added, telling everyone about our encounter with Victoria and Miss Rutherford.

"Unbelievable," said Claudia. "And this from someone who used to think all Americans sounded like cowboys."

"She was only like that at first," I pointed out. "It didn't take her too long to get used to everything here."

"Yeah," Logan agreed. "Don't you remember that last fall she wanted to go to more football games than I did? And that's saying a lot."

"No kidding," said Claudia dryly. Logan grinned.

"Well, we'll have to be extra sensitive to Victoria's feelings when we sit for her," Kristy said.

"Right," I said.

"Right-o," echoed Claudia in her best English accent.

Kristy leaned back in her chair. "Speaking of traveling abroad, I do have some news. It just so happens that I heard there's going to be another school trip this summer."

"You mean like the one to Hawaii?" I asked.

"Yup."

"Cool!" said Stacey. "Where to?"

"Oh, I hope it's someplace like Hawaii," Abby interrupted. "Someplace with lots of sun and great beaches."

"And gorgeous surfers," Stacey added.

"*I* hope this time we go to a big city, maybe someplace like Paris," said Claudia.

"I'd settle for the Wild West," Logan interjected.

"Which isn't all that wild anymore," Jessi reminded us.

"Where did you say we were going?" Stacey asked again.

"I don't know," Kristy admitted, laughing. "We'll probably hear more tomorrow at school."

We could hardly wait to find out.

CHAPTER 3

"I can't believe Ms. Frost is introducing logarithms now, only two days before the final," Abby grumbled. (Abby and I both have Ms. Frost for math, even though we're not in the same math class.) We were in the locker room, getting ready for gym.

"I know," I said. "But at least she said they won't be on the final."

Abby pulled out her sneakers and gym bag and slammed her locker door closed. "She told us that too. But why isn't she just reviewing the material that *will* be on the final, the way most teachers do?"

"Abby, cheer up," Stacey said. Her locker is near ours, and she had heard most of the conversation.

"Easy for you to say, Miss Math Whiz," said Abby, but she was smiling.

Stacey grinned. "You know the school trip Kristy was telling us about?" she asked.

25

"Yeah," Abby and I answered in unison.

"Well, Ms. Levine says it's official." (Ms. Levine is Stacey's homeroom teacher.) "All the homeroom teachers are going to give out the information this afternoon."

"Girls, hurry, I want you in the gym by the time the second bell rings," Mrs. Rosenauer, my least favorite gym teacher, interrupted.

"Right," said Abby, who was already dressed for class. (Gym is Abby's favorite subject.)

"Coming," I muttered as I pulled my T-shirt over my head.

Stacey was not the only one who had heard about the class trip. During the warm-up exercises, Cokie Mason told Erica Blumberg she thought the school was going to offer a trip to Alaska.

"Alaska?"

Cokie nodded.

Erica looked disappointed. "I was hoping for, I don't know, maybe Europe or something."

"What?" said Cokie, who couldn't hear Erica over the sound of the class doing calisthenics. "One-two-three-four. One-two-three-four," we chanted.

"I said Europe," Erica repeated, panting. "One-two-three-four."

"We're going to Europe?" Cokie sounded very surprised.

"Quiet!" Mrs. Rosenauer blew her whistle. "How many times do I have to tell you girls not to talk during the warm-up exercises? You need to concentrate on your breathing. Now, fifty sit-ups, please."

I groaned.

Luckily, we were not kept in suspense about the trip for long. A special homeroom period was scheduled after gym to talk about the trip and other "summer opportunities." As soon as I walked into my homeroom with Abby, I saw a stack of shiny brochures on our teacher's desk.

"Class, please take your seats," Mr. Blake was saying. "I have some exciting news."

Abby gave me a thumbs-up sign before we rushed to sit down.

"I know you have heard rumors about a school trip," Mr. Blake was saying as he held a stack of brochures. "Well, it's true. If you sign up by July first, you can travel to . . ."

We all leaned forward in our seats.

"I'll give you a hint," said Mr. Blake. The class groaned.

"Oh, just tell us," pleaded Katie Shea.

Instead of answering, Mr. Blake began to hum something that sounded like an anthem.

"Switzerland?" guessed Mary Sherwood.

"Close," said Mr. Blake, obviously enjoying himself.

Close to Switzerland, I thought. "Spain?" I squeaked.

"Canada!"

"The French Alps."

"Chez Maurice in downtown Stoneybrook!"

Everyone cracked up.

Mr. Blake rolled his eyes. "All right, class. I was humming 'Rule Britannia,' as well as France's anthem, which is 'La Marseillaise.' "

"La what?" asked Brad Simon.

"England and France! The class trip is to England and France!" I blurted out. I was so excited I barely realized I had called out until Mr. Blake congratulated me. Then I turned bright red.

"Correct, Mary Anne, England and France it is, specifically, London and Paris."

"London! Paris! All right!" shouted a bunch of kids.

"Well, it's not going to be as sunny as Hawaii," Abby whispered to me, "but it should be exciting. I've always wanted to go to Europe."

"Me too," I agreed.

"Will we get to see the dweebs with the furry helmets?" asked Rodge Somerset. (Rodge is a good friend of Alan Gray's. Need I say more?)

"If you are referring to the guards at Buckingham Palace," answered Mr. Blake, "yes, you will." He flipped through the brochure.

"What about the Queen?" Kate asked.

"If she is in residence, you might see her."

"I wonder if she gives autographs," Rodge muttered.

"Now, class," Mr. Blake was saying, "the procedure for this trip will be similar to last year's, meaning fifty students can sign up by July first. If fewer than fifty students sign up, the school will take names from the waiting list of nonstudents."

"How much does this trip cost?" Brad asked.

"For students, counting the discount, it will be four hundred dollars per person. All the information is in your brochure."

"Wow, that's cheaper than going to Hawaii," Abby pointed out.

Mr. Blake nodded. "Yes, because the airfare is less."

"It's still a lot of money," Brad muttered.

I nodded. I was excited about London and Paris. The brochure made the cities look so exciting with its photos of rose gardens, palaces, stone towers, and narrow winding streets. But I was worried about two things:

One. The trip cost a lot. Last time, it had been a stretch for my family to send Dawn and me, even though we did raise half our fare.

Two. What about Dawn? Would she be able to be taken from the waiting list? (Last year, her name came up at the last minute). Judging by how excited my homeroom sounded, there might be more interest in London and Paris than in Hawaii.

As soon as homeroom was over, Abby cried, "Oh, Mary Anne! I'm soooo excited about London, especially. My mom spent her junior year of college at London University. She still talks about what a great time she had there, and the theater, galleries, and especially the bookstores." (Abby's mother works as an editor for a big publishing company in New York.)

Luckily, Abby was too excited to notice how worried and quiet I was, which was just as well. Unlike her, I still wasn't sure I wanted to go.

"But Mary Anne," Kristy said at the Baby-sitters Club meeting the next day, "if all your friends are going to Europe, you have to want to go."

"Let the girl decide for herself," Claudia said as she handed me a bag of salt-and-vinegar potato chips.

"I'm not trying to decide for her," Kristy said sharply.

I bit into a chip. "It's Dawn I'm worried about," I explained. "If she can go, I'll go too."

Kristy frowned. That was not the answer she'd been hoping for. Luckily, just at that moment, the phone rang. Claudia snatched it up.

"Hello. Baby-sitters Club," she said. "Oh, hello, Mrs. Simon."

The rest of us sat up and looked at one another. Why was a teacher calling us?

"Really," Claudia was saying, "I'm sure we would all be interested."

"What?" Kristy mouthed.

"I'll talk to them and call you right back," said Claudia as she put the phone down.

"What was that about?" asked Stacey.

Claudia grinned and leaned back against her big red pillows.

"That," she answered dramatically, "was Mrs. Simon."

"We know," said Kristy.

"Well, Stoneybrook Elementary School is going to have a playground camp this summer for kids from the neighborhood."

"What a great idea," Abby commented.

"They need counselors," Claudia continued. "Mrs. Simon was wondering if any of us would be interested."

What a question. We were all interested — *very* interested.

Claudia lost no time calling Mrs. Simon back. "Ask her if they need a softball coach," Kristy whispered, while Claudia listened to Mrs. Simon.

"Or someone to teach soccer," Abby said. She didn't even bother to whisper.

Claudia looked at them and rolled her eyes. (She dislikes sports almost as much as I do.)

"Yes," Claudia said to Mrs. Simon. "Right." (Long pause.) "Okay. We'll look tomorrow, then."

"Look for what?" Kristy asked after Claudia hung up.

"Mrs. Simon said the playground information will be posted on the job board at school tomorrow," Claudia answered.

"All right," said Kristy. "Why didn't you ask her about a softball coach?"

"Yeah," Abby chimed in.

Claudia shook her head and threw one of her pillows in their direction. "Don't you two ever think about anything but sports?"

We all laughed . . . and made plans to check the bulletin board first thing in the morning.

CHAPTER 4

The next day, most of us came to school early so we could look at the bulletin board in the main hallway. Kristy was already reading the board along with plenty of other kids when I arrived. I inched my way up so I could see. Being short does not help in these situations.

"Hi, Mary Anne," Kristy greeted me. She pointed to a big notice calling for playground counselors. I saw that there were six positions open for students from Stoneybrook Middle School. (Yesss!) There were also positions open for older kids.

Playground Camp would start on July first and run to the end of August. That meant employment for most of the summer. Applications were due a few days after school was out, so we could work on them after finals. (Whew.) Interviews would be held in two weeks.

"Sounds good," I said.

"Very," Kristy agreed. She was already copying down information in her notebook.

Next to the notice about the playground jobs was a huge picture of Big Ben and the Eiffel Tower with information about the trip to Europe. (No wonder the hallway was so crowded.) The trip would begin July fifteenth and run until July twenty-third. Uh-oh.

"We can't be hired as counselors if we're going to miss nine days of work, can we?" I asked Kristy.

Kristy shrugged. "I don't think that should be a problem."

"You don't?"

"No," Kristy said. "The trip is nine full days. That means we'll only be missing one work-week. We can probably ask for that time off." Kristy sounded very sure of this. I, however, had my doubts.

"Oooh," squealed Cokie, who had just seen the board. "These playground jobs sound perfect. It's hard to get summer jobs at our age because everyone wants the high school kids. I'm definitely applying."

"Me too," Katie Shea said.

"Hey, get this," Howie Johnson was saying to Brad Simon. "We'll get paid to hang out at the playground all summer. My kind of job."

"No kidding," muttered Brad. "I just hope they hire both of us."

I hope they don't! I thought. There was going

to be a lot of competition for the playground jobs.

Kristy was not too worried. "Look, Mary Anne, we have more baby-sitting experience than anyone else who's applying," she said when most of the other kids were out of earshot.

"Except the other members of the BSC," I pointed out.

"You worry too much," Kristy stated as she headed off to take her English final. "Don't forget that Mrs. Simon called *us*. That probably means BSC members have more than a good chance."

Kristy did have a point.

I spent the rest of the morning taking my social studies final. By lunchtime, I had convinced myself that not everybody in the BSC would want the playground jobs. I figured Jessi and Mallory might not apply. Logan was too busy with sports. So was Abby. And Shannon was going to summer camp. That left Kristy, Claudia, Stacey, and me — four of us for six slots. Perfect. There might even be room for Dawn if she wanted a job. Knowing Dawn, she probably would. Now all I had to worry about was whether Dawn and I would get jobs together, right?

Wrong!

By midday, things began to get a little complicated. First, I met up with Mallory in the bathroom.

"Don't those playground jobs sound perfect?" she asked as she brushed her hair and tied it back.

"Yeah, they do," I said a little warily.

"Jessi and I are definitely sending in applications," Mallory continued. "I just hope we won't be disqualified because we're too young."

"The jobs are open to anyone from SMS," I assured her. But I was feeling worried again. That meant seven BSC members would be applying for six spots, if Dawn applied.

Then, on the lunch line, Logan told me *he* was interested in a playground job.

"What about all your sports and your job at the Rosebud Cafe?" I asked. I helped myself to the macaroni and cheese, even though I wasn't very hungry.

"This job pays more," Logan answered. "Besides, I'd rather be outside than clearing tables in the summer."

"Oh," I said in a small voice.

"Mary Anne, what's the matter? I thought you'd be happy. If we both get jobs, we can spend more time together this summer."

"I know. It's just that I'm afraid there's going to be a lot of competition."

"But BSC members are experienced."

I nodded. Sometimes Logan sounded just like Kristy.

"So, guys, did you see the information on the playground jobs?" Abby asked when we reached the lunch table.

"You applying?" Logan inquired.

"You bet."

"But I thought you wanted to go to Europe," I said.

"No reason I can't do both," Abby answered. "Kristy doesn't think Mrs. Simon will mind if we take a week off."

"But if we all take that same week off, she *will* mind," I pointed out.

Abby shrugged and opened her lunchbox. "She might be able to find some replacements for that week."

I shook my head.

Soon I had more reason to worry. By the time lunch was over, I had learned that at least twelve kids were applying for the playground jobs, including Kristy, Abby, Stacey, Logan, Claudia, and me. And that was just from the eighth grade. Including Jessi and Mallory, there would be nine BSC members competing for only six spots. Groan.

With that kind of competition, I wasn't sure how Dawn would do. And judging by how many kids were talking about going to London and Paris, it didn't seem too likely Dawn would get off the waiting list this time. I sighed. Even before school was over, it was turning out to be a *very* complicated summer.

CHAPTER 5

Saturday

Three things you should know about Vicki right now:

1) Call her Vicki — only.

2) She wants to see as much of Mary Anne as she can before she leaves. (So, if you're baby-sitting, and you're not Mary Anne, be prepared.)

3) Don't take her on any more tours of the neighborhood, though it seemed like a brilliant idea at the time, if I do say so myself.

It was Saturday afternoon when Kristy set off to baby-sit for Victoria (I mean Vicki). Perhaps what happened was my fault, but Kristy says I shouldn't blame myself so much, that I really had nothing to do with what Kristy called "one of her worst baby-sitting jobs ever."

You see, I was the one who was supposed to baby-sit for Victoria. Of all of us, I had sat for her the most, and Miss Rutherford requested me specifically when she called to make the arrangements. I did accept, but then I found out that Dawn's plane was coming in at the same time, and I wanted to be at the airport to meet her. So I called Kristy, who said she would take my place.

I guess my first mistake was that I didn't call Victoria too. . . .

When Kristy arrived at Victoria's mansion, the butler ushered her into the spacious front parlor. "Miss Rutherford will be right with you," he announced.

Miss Rutherford bustled into the parlor soon after. "Hello, Kristy. Where is Mary Anne?" she asked.

"At the airport, picking up Dawn."

"Oh." Miss Rutherford sounded — and looked — distracted. "Well, thank goodness one of you is here. I'm at my wit's end."

"Really? What's the matter?"

"It's Victoria. I just don't know what to do about her. She's so depressed about moving. All she does is sit in front of the telly, watching reruns of those dreadful American programs. And she's grieving for all the friends she's made here."

"I'll see if I can get her mind on something else," Kristy offered.

"Oh, that would be wonderful. Perhaps you could take her outside. She looks wan from staying indoors." Miss Rutherford was wringing her hands as she walked Kristy to the playroom. "It's not only the television. She refuses to wear anything but the sloppiest clothes. She won't even put on decent shoes anymore. And she won't answer to any name other than Vicki."

Kristy could barely keep herself from laughing.

Miss Rutherford shook her head. "I don't know what her parents are going to think. They come home tomorrow." (Victoria's parents, Sir Charles and Lady Kent, were often away on business.)

As soon as she stepped into the playroom, Kristy registered Victoria's mood. She was sitting on a big pillow in front of the TV, wearing denim shorts, a T-shirt with the slogan "Let's Go Mets" on it, and no shoes. Her shiny brown hair was tied back in a ponytail.

The room looked different too. Pennants of sports teams hung on the walls, covering the Beatrix Potter wallpaper. Victoria's English Tudor dollhouse was now in a corner gathering dust. Before, it had been in the center of the room. Stacks of Marvel comic books, a Slinky, Gumby dolls, and a pair of in-line skates were scattered in front of the large overstuffed couch.

"Hello, Vicki," Kristy said brightly.

Victoria listlessly turned away from the TV, which was playing a rerun of *The Dick Van Dyke Show.*

"Oh, hi, Kristy. Is Mary Anne coming later?"

When Kristy explained where I was, Victoria looked even more unhappy. "But we distinctly asked for Mary Anne, didn't we?"

"Yes, dear," Miss Rutherford said soothingly. "But Mary Anne had no way of knowing about her sister's plane."

Victoria's shoulders sagged. "But I'm the one who's leaving," she said, pouting, as tears welled in her blue eyes. "Doesn't Mary Anne want to see me as much as she can before I go?"

"Sure she does," Kristy said. "We all do. But you know what?"

"What?" Victoria still sounded listless.

"The BSC members are visiting London this

summer on a school trip. We could all come and visit you."

"Oh, would you?" Victoria gave Kristy her full attention. "Could you stay at my home? We have plenty of room."

"I don't see why not," Kristy said, grinning at the idea of sleeping overnight in an old manor house. "We'd probably need to get permission from the tour leaders, but I'm sure they would let us."

"Oh, lovely — I mean *great*." Victoria smiled for the first time.

"And you know what else," Kristy continued as she sat down beside Victoria. "Karen would like to see you. Would you like to come over and play at my house?" (Kristy's stepsister, Karen, is seven; she and Victoria had become friends.)

"Oh, I would love to see Karen," Victoria murmured in reply. "I'm going to miss all my friends in the States so much."

As much as she wanted to see Karen, it took much persuasion to get Victoria to leave her TV program. "You know, we don't have *The Dick Van Dyke Show* in England. I just love American TV," Victoria said as they walked outside. (Before they left, Victoria put on a pair of sandals. Miss Rutherford insisted.)

Karen was in Kristy's front yard, playing

with David Michael (Kristy's brother, age seven) and their neighbors Hannie and Linny Papadakis (who are seven and nine, respectively). As soon as they saw Victoria, they rushed to her.

"Victoria!" Karen shrieked.

"It's Vicki," Victoria reminded her.

"You changed your name?" asked Linny.

Victoria glared. "I just prefer Vicki."

"I like Victoria better," said Hannie.

"Call her what she wants," Kristy jumped in. "It's her name."

"Oh, I wish you were not leaving, Vicki," Karen interjected.

"I wish I weren't either." Victoria sniffled. "I am going to miss all of you so much."

"Do you have a cold?" David Michael asked. Linny looked embarrassed. Kristy thought it was time to change the subject. "Why don't we all take a walk around the neighborhood?" she suggested.

"Yes," said Hannie. "That way, Victor — I mean Vicki — can see all her favorite places."

"And say good-bye to them," Karen added. (Karen is a stickler for proper good-byes.)

"I don't want to say good-bye," said Victoria, sniffling more loudly.

Kristy gave Karen a Look. "You won't have to say good-bye."

"Do you need a tissue?" David Michael asked Victoria.

Kristy's older brother Charlie agreed to drive them on a "Stoneybrook Tour." The first stop was the Papadakises' house across the street, so Hannie and Linny could ask their parents if it was okay to go for a ride. (It was.)

"Next stop, Stoneybrook Day School," Kristy announced.

"You should be a tour leader," said David Michael.

"She's practicing for her trip to Europe," Karen said.

Stoneybrook Day School looks like a college campus. Four very old redbrick buildings are set around an enormous grass courtyard. The buildings are connected by covered walkways in the front.

Karen and Linny headed for the courtyard. The others followed. School was out for the summer, but many people in the neighborhood came to the courtyard on weekends to read, play, walk their dogs, or sit in the sun.

"Look at those two collies!" Hannie shouted, pointing enthusiastically.

"They're gorgeous," Kristy commented as the dogs came toward them. A girl who looked to be about ten years old was holding their leashes.

"Whoa," said Linny as one of the collies jumped up on him.

"Pebbles, heel," their owner commanded. But Pebbles paid no attention. Linny laughed and stroked the dog's soft fur.

"Ooh, I just love dogs," said Hannie as she patted the other one, who had just started growling.

"Why is she growling?" asked Karen.

"Bam-Bam, stop it!" said the owner. But Bam-Bam only growled more loudly and moved toward Victoria.

"Aaaugh!" Victoria shouted, hiding behind Kristy. She had turned quite pale.

"What's the matter, Vicki? She won't hurt you," Karen insisted. At that moment, Pebbles let go of Linny and decided to jump on Victoria instead.

"No!" shrieked Victoria, pushing Pebbles away. "NO. KRISTY, HELP ME! AAAUGH!"

By now Pebbles was licking Victoria's face and Bam-Bam was still growling.

"Pebbles, get down," her owner shouted, yanking the dog away. "And Bam-Bam, stop that growling! I'm very sorry about this," the girl said to Kristy.

"It's all right. We'll just move along," Kristy said, gently leading Victoria away.

"I'm dreadfully frightened — I mean, scared

stiff of dogs," Victoria explained. "I was bitten by one when I was younger."

"That could be why the collie growled at you," said Karen. "Dogs can tell when people don't like them."

"Then why was the other one so friendly?" David Michael wanted to know.

Karen shrugged. "Maybe she was hoping to change Victoria's mind." At that, Victoria actually smiled — thinly.

"I have an idea," Karen said, pointing to the left. "Let's walk by the stream." The stream was one of Karen and Hannie's favorite hangouts. Whenever they went there, they liked to pretend they were at the beach or camping out by the water.

"Okay," Kristy said. "But don't get your shoes wet."

"Let's pretend we're shipwrecked pirates on an island!" Linny shouted.

"Yes!" David Michael agreed. "And here's my pirate's sword." He grabbed a stick and waved it in front of him.

"I'll get you, Bluebeard," Karen shouted as she too found a stick and waved it in front of David Michael's nose. "You stole all my gold doubloons." (Incidentally, Karen has a wonderful imagination.)

"Hark, there is our mighty ship," said Victoria, who loved games like this. She pointed to a plastic sailboat someone had left by the side of the stream.

"Shiver me timbers!" Karen yelled. (Karen had been reading a lot of pirate books lately.) "Let us see if we can sail away and escape the evil Bluebeard and his skipper, Captain, uh, Captain . . ."

"Captain Blood!" Victoria finished for her.

"Right. Captain Blood," said Karen, running toward the stream. The boat lay on the other side, so Karen had to cross the stream by stepping on a couple of big rocks in the streambed.

Victoria chased after her, but her sandals didn't grip the rocks as well as Karen's sneakers had.

"Victoria, be careful!" Kristy called out.

But it was too late. Victoria slipped and splashed into the stream.

"Oh, no!" Kristy shouted as she rushed to Victoria. "Are you all right?"

Other than a scraped knee and elbow, Victoria wasn't hurt, just shaken and sopping wet.

"Come on, I'll take you right home," Kristy said.

"But the game," Victoria spluttered.

"We can play another time," Karen said as she handed Victoria the plastic sailboat.

At this point Victoria, who had been sniffling all morning, finally burst into tears. "But I don't want to leave my friends or this game," she wailed after Kristy and Charlie had driven everyone back home, and Kristy left her safely with Miss Rutherford, who tried not to seem too shocked by Victoria's bedraggled appearance.

"She's so upset about this move," Miss Rutherford explained after Victoria was out of earshot, in the hot bath Miss Rutherford had insisted she take.

Kristy nodded.

"I just hope the poor dear recovers soon." Miss Rutherford was shaking her head.

Kristy hoped so too. Otherwise, it was going to be a very sad — and hard — good-bye.

CHAPTER 6

"Oh, Mary Anne, it looks gorgeous in here!" Stacey exclaimed.

"I couldn't have done it better myself," Claudia said, referring to the banner that read "Welcome Home" hanging over Dawn's bed.

I must admit, Dawn's room did look good. The sun shone through the small round window near the ceiling. Her bed was covered with a soft white quilt and piled high with blue and green pillows — as well as presents from Sharon, Dad, and me. A light rug partially covered the hardwood floor. Posters of tropical fish and sunny beaches hung on the walls. A bulletin board was studded with Dawn's collection of ecology buttons that declared "Save the Whales," "Save the Beaches," "Recycle." (Dawn is passionate about conserving the environment.)

"I just love this room," Stacey said as she

looked around. "It's so cool the secret passage from the barn leads right here."

"Girls, we're almost ready to leave," Dad called from downstairs.

"Coming!" I shouted back.

Stacey, Claudia, and I were going to the airport to pick up Dawn and Jeff. Actually everyone in the BSC had wanted to come but Kristy, Jessi, and Mallory were baby-sitting, and Abby had a soccer game. So it was just going to be the three of us, plus Sharon and Dad, of course. Luckily, Dad's new van was big enough for all of us.

"I can't believe we're going to be seeing Dawn in less than two hours," Stacey said.

"I can't either," I admitted. I was so excited that I shivered a little just thinking about it. It seemed like forever since I'd last seen Dawn.

When Dawn first told me she was moving back to California for good, I was hurt and angry. I could not believe she would want to live so far away from me. Luckily, we had a good talk before she left, and I realized she had made the choice that was right for her. Since she's been gone, we've made an effort to write each other regularly. I know all about Dawn's life, and she knows all about mine. Even though we've lost the closeness that comes with living together, our friendship has adapted to the move. Dawn once told me that the friendships that survive long distances are sometimes the truest friendships, because the friends care enough to make the effort to keep in touch. And we certainly do.

"Mary Anne, are you almost ready?" Dad called again.

"Yeah!" I shouted back as we all headed out of Dawn's room.

"What does Dawn think about going to Europe this summer?" Stacey asked me as we ran downstairs.

"I haven't told her yet," I confessed.

"You haven't?" Claudia was amazed. "Don't you phone each other all the time?"

"At least once a week," I answered. "And we write a lot. But we've both been really busy with finals. And lately we've mostly just talked about Gracie. Dawn's kind of upset that she has to leave Gracie so soon after she was born."

"Yeah," said Stacey. "I'd feel the same way."

"Hello, girls," Sharon said when we walked in the kitchen. Dad was fishing his car keys out of his pocket. Sharon was opening the door to the refrigerator.

"Can you think of something else we should pick up for Dawn and Jeff? I think I have all their favorite foods," Sharon said.

I laughed. Sharon had gone food shopping

after dinner the night before and had come home with a large supply of tofu, tahini, tabbouleh, pita bread, and plenty of fresh fruits and vegetables.

"Dawn food," Claudia muttered, looking suspiciously into the refrigerator with me. "I think you might have missed the apple-mango-guava-papaya juice."

"We might be able to stop on the way home," Dad said. "But right now, let's go. We don't want to be late and keep Dawn and Jeff waiting."

"No chance of that," Sharon said, laughing. "We're almost two hours early." But she locked her arm in Dad's and walked out to the van, beaming. Sharon looks so happy whenever Dawn and Jeff come to visit. I think Dad is happy too, but he doesn't show his feelings as much.

"Next stop, the airport," Dad announced after we had piled into the van.

Dawn's plane turned out to be ten minutes early. We arrived even earlier, but we managed to find plenty to do. I was the first one to spot Dawn and Jeff walking through the gate.

"Dawn!" I shouted, waving wildly. (I don't usually behave that way in public places.)

"Dawn!" Stacey and Claudia shrieked. We almost knocked over some passengers in our mad rush to greet her.

"It's so great to see you!" Dawn shouted, hugging us, then Sharon.

"Oh, Mom," she said, on the verge of tears. Sharon was already crying as she embraced Dawn, then Jeff, then both of them.

"Jeff, I believe you've grown some more," Sharon announced, stepping back to get a good look.

"You *always* say that." Jeff groaned, turning red. But he looked pleased.

"I'm starving," Dawn announced as we waited at the baggage claim for her luggage.

"Me too," Jeff chimed in. "We only got these disgusting sandwiches and cookies on the plane for lunch."

"Well, first stop before home will be Cabbages and Kings," Dad said.

"Great!" Dawn beamed. Cabbages and Kings is her favorite restaurant in Stoneybrook, because it serves only natural foods: whole-grain breads, natural fruit juices, and wonderful tofu dishes (according to Dawn).

Needless to say, Cabbages and Kings is not Claudia's idea of a great restaurant. But she was so happy to see Dawn that she didn't even make a face when Dawn ordered the daily special: eggplant casserole.

The rest of us hid our grins. "I'll have that too," I told the waitress.

After our food came, Dawn and Jeff passed around the latest pictures of Gracie, who was only a couple of weeks old. After we were through oohing and ahhing, I turned to Dawn.

"We have something to tell you," I said, looking at Claudia and Stacey.

"Yes, we have a lot to tell you," Stacey said.

"What?" Dawn asked. Sharon, Dad, and Jeff looked at us with raised eyebrows.

"Well, to begin with," I said, "there are these jobs open for playground counselors." (Dad and Sharon already knew all about the playground jobs since I had been talking of little else at home.)

"You mean we would be baby-sitting outside all summer?" Dawn sounded thrilled. (She's an outdoors freak too.)

"Correct," I said.

"Are there openings for campers?" asked Jeff. "Are JAB going?" (JAB is Jeff's nickname for the Pike triplets — Jordan, Adam, and Byron — his best friends in Stoneybrook.)

"You know, I didn't even think to ask," I said. "But they might be. Mallory wants to be a playground counselor."

"Jeff, what a good idea," Sharon said. "Playground camp would be perfect for you."

"*If* JAB go too," Jeff insisted. While he talked some more with his mother, I filled Dawn in on the playground jobs. "The only drawback," I explained, "is that there's going to be a lot of competition for these jobs."

"I can see why," Dawn said. "They sound perfect. And I would love to get one. I haven't been doing too much baby-sitting lately. Even with Gracie. Carol and Mrs. Bruen have been doing most of the baby work."

"I wouldn't worry too much about getting a playground job," Stacey assured us. "You know, Mrs. Simon *asked* the BSC members to apply. That gives us an edge."

"I hope," said Dawn. (I decided this would not be the time to point out that now nine of us were applying for only six openings.)

"But wait — there's more exciting news," Stacey said, beaming. "More exciting than the playground jobs, in my opinion."

"Tell me," Dawn said, putting down her fork.

"Well . . ." Stacey paused dramatically, her eyes sparkling. "There's another school trip."

"Oh?" was all Dawn said.

"To London, isn't that right, mates?" Stacey spoke in a fake English accent.

"And Par-eee," Claudia answered in an equally fake French accent.

I laughed. Then Claudia, Stacey, and I started talking about the trip and Victoria and how we might be able to visit Victoria in her manor house.

It took us awhile to realize that Dawn wasn't saying anything. In fact, the more we talked about Europe, the more subdued she became. She had even stopped eating. To be honest, Sharon and Jeff didn't look too happy either.

"Is anything the matter?" I finally asked.

"Well," Dawn began, choosing her words carefully, "I was hoping to stay in Stoneybrook for the whole summer."

"I was hoping you would too," Sharon said, looking relieved.

Dawn sighed. "This is my first trip to Connecticut since Christmas. Since I'm not here that much anymore, it doesn't feel right to leave, even for only nine or ten days."

I nodded. I certainly understood. I had been looking forward to spending a lot of time with Dawn too.

I looked at Stacey and Claudia. Stacey could not hide her disappointment. Claudia was moving her eggplant from one side of the plate to the other. She didn't look as upset as Stacey did. In fact, it was hard to tell what she was thinking. The only thing that was obvious was that she hated eggplant.

I sighed. Now that Dawn wasn't going to Europe, I wasn't sure what I should do.

CHAPTER 7

"Ta-da!" Mallory and Jessi sang together. Between them, they carried a tray filled with carrot sticks, slices of pita bread, and a bowl of hummus into our Monday BSC meeting. Hummus is made from chickpeas, garlic, lemon juice, and tahini. And how do I know that? By watching Dawn make it countless times in our kitchen. She'd even made a batch this weekend.

"What a way to welcome Dawn back," Kristy said.

"Yeah, thanks, guys," Dawn said. She was sitting cross-legged on the floor between Abby and Shannon. The entire club had turned out for Dawn's "welcome home" meeting.

Claudia disappeared under her bed and emerged with a cellophane bag of Cheez Doodles. "Food we can eat," she announced as she passed the bag to Mallory.

Mallory laughed.

"I prefer Dawn's food," Abby announced as she dipped a carrot stick in the hummus.

"See," said Dawn, waving a piece of pita bread in the air. "The rest of you just don't know what you're missing."

"I do," said Claudia. "And I'll miss it, thank you."

"I guess no more eggplant casseroles for you," Stacey remarked.

"Right," Claudia answered.

"Oh, guys, you didn't have to," Dawn protested, as we began showering her with small gifts: a tie-dyed T-shirt from Claudia; dangly silver earrings from Stacey, who bought them in New York; a baseball cap from Kristy; a bottle of mango-kiwi juice from Logan; and a book of British ghost stories from Abby and Shannon.

"Oooh, I just love ghost stories," Dawn said as she opened her last present.

"And the best things about these," said Abby, "is you can read them on location."

Dawn and I exchanged glances. I knew that Dawn wanted to tell everyone she wasn't going to Europe. But just then, Kristy called the meeting to order.

"The first order of business," Kristy was saying, "is money."

"Money?" Dawn looked blank.

"Yes, money," Kristy said. "You know, the

stuff we're going to need to get us to Europe."

Abby nodded. "My mom said I can go if I raise half my plane fare."

"Mine said the same thing," Stacey said. "Same deal as when we went to Hawaii."

"How many of us are going to need to raise half the plane fare?" asked Kristy.

"Plus spending money," Stacey added.

I raised my hand. (I knew that if I went to Europe — and I still hadn't decided for sure whether I wanted to go — Dad would ask me to pay half. That's what he had insisted on for Hawaii.) Stacey, Abby, Kristy, Claudia, Jessi, and Logan had also raised their hands.

"I'm still trying to talk my parents into letting me go," said Mallory. (Mallory had not been able to go to Hawaii because the trip had cost too much.)

"At least this trip isn't as expensive," Jessi pointed out. "Oh, Mal, I hope you can go."

"Me too," Mallory said.

"What about you, Dawn?" Kristy asked.

"I'm not going," Dawn answered flatly.

"You're not going?" Kristy said. She did not look pleased.

"I can't go. I don't feel it's right to leave Stoneybrook when I'm not here very often anyway."

"Okay." Kristy sighed, still looking miffed. "That means, with the rest of us going, except maybe Mallory, we're going to need —"

"One thousand four hundred dollars," Stacey chimed in. "And that's not including spending money."

"Well, it's the summer," Abby pointed out. "We can baby-sit like crazy."

"We're going to need more than baby-sitting money," Stacey interjected.

"We could always wash cars and mow lawns like we did for Hawaii," Abby suggested.

"Seriously, guys," Kristy said. "We are going to have to do chores like that again. But as I recall, we did not make enough money mowing lawns."

"No, we didn't," Stacey agreed. "And the pay wasn't necessarily worth the time and effort we spent doing it."

"Does anyone have any other suggestions?" Kristy was getting impatient with us.

"What about a bake sale?" Jessi suggested.

Kristy did not look thrilled. She hates to cook even more than I do.

"Well, to be honest," said Dawn, "Mary Anne and I tried to have a food sale last time. We hardly earned anything."

"Were you selling food like that?" Claudia asked, pointing to Dawn's tray.

"Well, yes," Dawn admitted.

Claudia shook her head.

"You know," I began, "Dawn and I did make

a lot of money when we had a yard sale."

"That's right," Dawn said. "We collected all this junk around our house — old dolls and stuffed animals and books. Stuff I didn't think anyone would want. But it sold like crazy."

The room was quiet. I looked at Kristy. I could tell she was thinking.

"That's not a bad idea," Kristy said slowly.

"A junk sale?" Abby asked.

"No, not a junk sale exactly," Kristy answered. "But a sale with a theme. In the summer, people always seem to be cleaning out their houses. I think many of our clients' families would be happy to donate things they're not using anymore."

"Yeah," Shannon said. "It saves them a trip to the Salvation Army."

"But we need a theme," Kristy insisted.

I thought about Victoria and all the stuffed animals she hardly ever played with anymore because she thought they were for babies. Now that I thought about it, *I* still had some stuffed animals I didn't want anymore.

"What about a stuffed animal sale?" I suggested. "We could sell other things too, but that could be our theme."

"Yesss!" Kristy yelled, giving me the thumbs-up sign. "I like it."

"I know lots of kids who would be interested

in coming if that's how we advertised it," Mallory added.

"I know my parents want to get rid of some of my old stuffed animals," Jessi said. "They say I have an oversupply."

"Everyone does," Dawn commented, laughing.

"Well, I'm glad that's settled," Kristy said. "We can talk more about this later, but at least we have a good idea to work with." (To Kristy, ideas are everything.)

"I have to go to the bathroom," Dawn announced, just as the phone rang.

"All that mango juice," said Claudia as she picked up the phone. "Oh, hello, Mrs. Wilder. I'll see who's free, and I'll call you right back."

"Mrs. Wilder needs a sitter for Rosie this Wednesday from ten in the morning to one-thirty in the afternoon," Claudia announced.

I checked the appointment book. I was babysitting for Victoria. Mal and Jessi also had baby-sitting commitments. Shannon had a dress rehearsal. Abby and Logan were busy with soccer, since the summer league had officially begun. And Claudia had a pottery lesson. "Kristy, Dawn, and Stacey are the only ones free," I said.

"I'll take it," Stacey volunteered.

I carefully wrote her name in the appointment book while Claudia called Mrs. Wilder back.

When I looked up, I noticed Kristy staring at me. "Mary Anne," she began, "I was just thinking, if Dawn is definitely not going to Europe, does that mean you're going to stay behind too?"

Kristy's question caught me by surprise. I could feel myself blushing, and I hated that. My friends were all looking at me. Dawn was still in the bathroom. "Uh," I said, "I haven't decided yet."

Kristy did not look pleased. I knew that wasn't the answer she wanted to hear.

"You know," said Logan, "I, uh, haven't decided for sure if I'm going to go either."

"You guys!" Abby protested.

Kristy was looking more and more huffy. The others seemed downright disappointed. "Well, I hope you decide soon," Kristy said crossly. "It'll affect how much money we have to raise."

"Speaking of money," Abby added, "don't forget the playground jobs. We'll be making more on the playground than we normally do when we baby-sit."

"*If* we all get jobs," Jessi reminded us, as Dawn walked into the room and sat next to her.

"Applications are due in two days," I pointed out.

Kristy nodded grimly.

Everyone was suddenly very quiet. We had even stopped eating. Usually when we apply for something, we all help each other. But now no one was offering up any suggestions. We'd suddenly become each other's competition. (I hate that word, and I hated the feeling in the room. I wished someone would say something.)

"I don't know if the people going to Europe will be able to be counselors," Dawn said delicately. "Is Mrs. Simon going to let you miss a week of work?"

"I talked with Mrs. Simon," Kristy reported huffily. "She said the time off won't automatically disqualify us."

"Whew." Abby sighed loudly.

"*But*," Kristy continued, "it will be taken into account when the final decisions are made."

"Oh." Abby and Stacey groaned together.

"Maybe it's a good thing I might be staying here," Mallory joked. "I'll probably have a better chance."

"Don't count on it," Kristy snapped. "If anyone has a *better chance*, it will be the older members of the BSC."

"How would you know?" Jessi asked.

"I just think that given the choice, Mrs. Simon would probably want to hire eighth-graders over sixth-graders."

"Well, excuse me," muttered Mal.

"*You* don't seem to think we're too young to baby-sit," Jessi pointed out.

"Yeah," Mallory added, sounding angry, "if you think we're such babies, why did you invite us into your club in the first place?"

Kristy shrugged. "I don't think you're too young, but Mrs. Simon might."

"Maybe it would be better to let Mrs. Simon decide without second-guessing her," Stacey suggested.

"I'm not trying to second-guess Mrs. Simon," Kristy snapped. "Geez, you guys, what is this?"

"Well, I, for one, don't particularly like the way you're talking to us," Claudia said.

"Okay, I'm sorry," Kristy answered gruffly. "Does anyone have any other business to bring up?"

No one did.

I was relieved when Kristy said the meeting was adjourned.

Later that night, I was in my room, working on my application. I planned to write a rough draft before I went to sleep, so I would have plenty of time to think about what I had said and maybe rewrite it. (I'm very organized that way.) So far I had filled out boring information such as my name, date of birth, address, and phone number. In the section asking about previous counseling experience, I wrote a short essay about my work at a circus camp. In the section covering previous work with children, I wrote a long essay about the BSC and my role in it. Then I came to the part where I got stuck:

I had to indicate whether I was available for the whole summer.

I walked around the room. I petted Tigger. Then I sat down at my desk again.

I checked the box that said "yes."

I *would* be available the entire summer. I was not going to Europe. I wanted to stay in Stoneybrook with Dawn. And that was final.

CHAPTER 8

After that awful Monday meeting, Stacey, Kristy, and Claudia lost no time lining up garden-care jobs. And they enlisted Dawn and me to help. For all they knew, I was still going to Europe.

On Tuesday, Dawn and I mowed two lawns and weeded four flower beds. Logan worked an extra shift at the Rosebud Cafe and also mowed lawns. On Wednesday, Dawn and I each were going to baby-sitting jobs before our afternoon BSC meeting. (Now that school was over, there were plenty of sitting jobs during the day.)

I was glad we were so busy. It kept us from having to talk about the playground jobs, which were making everyone tense and competitive. On Tuesday, when I asked Claudia if she'd finished her application, she didn't even answer me. And when I suggested to Kristy that we might want to read each other's application essays, she became very annoyed. "No way, Mary Anne," she had said. "This has to be our own work."

Kristy's answer had made me mad. Did she think I was going to steal her ideas? I just find it helpful to talk things over with her. Usually Kristy likes doing that too. But not for these jobs. And if that was the way she wanted to be, fine. Kristy is *so* competitive.

"Hey, Dawn, wake up," I said, grinning at her from the doorway of her bedroom. It was after nine o'clock on Wednesday morning, and she had a baby-sitting job in less than two hours. (At least Dawn and I weren't mad at each other.)

"Yeah," Jeff said. He was in Dawn's doorway too. "You sure don't live up to your name." (This is a joke Jeff makes a lot.)

Dawn threw a pillow at her brother.

"Kristy just called," I reported as I sat down on Dawn's bed. "She thought it would be fun if we all went to Pizza Express after the meeting."

"Really?" Dawn sounded surprised. "Can we afford it? I mean, aren't you guys supposed to be saving money for Europe?"

"Uh, yeah," I said. (I hadn't told Dawn about my plans to stay in Stoneybrook. I wanted to break the news to Kristy first.) "I asked Kristy about that too, and she said she thought it would be fun for us, and we could plan the fund-raiser over dinner."

"That's true," Dawn agreed. "Besides, it might be a good way to relieve all this tension about the playground jobs."

I nodded. I knew just what Dawn meant.

"What's so tense about working on a playground?" Jeff wanted to know.

"Getting the job," Dawn answered. "A lot of people are applying."

"I sure hope there aren't a lot of people applying to be campers," Jeff said as he bounded out of the room. "Dawn, you know, breakfast is ready and it's one of your favorites — organic whole wheat waffles with strawberries."

"Yum," said Dawn, getting out of bed.

That was the morning. The afternoon brought Victoria.

"Mary Anne, are you leaving already? But you've only just arrived," Victoria was grumbling.

Actually I had "only just arrived" two hours earlier. Since then, Victoria and I had watched one *Star Trek* rerun, played Scrabble, and taken a walk in the rose garden behind her house.

"If I don't leave now, Vicki, I'll be late for the BSC meeting."

"Oh, bother. I mean, oh give me a break. You

spend more time at your meetings than you do with me."

I decided this was not the time to tell Victoria that if it weren't for those "meetings," we would never have met each other in the first place. "You know how Kristy is if anyone is late," I said as I grabbed my bag and started to walk with Victoria down the long hallway that eventually led to the front door.

That made Victoria giggle — a little. "Well, at least I'll be seeing you in London. I can't wait for you to see my house."

"Uh, right," I muttered. (I know, I know. I should have told Victoria I wasn't going on the trip, but I didn't want to cause a scene just when I was leaving.)

"See you soon," was all I said as I stooped down to kiss her good-bye.

" 'Bye, Mary Anne. Come visit me tomorrow."

Victoria stood in her doorway, waving to me, until I was out of sight. I waved back until I was around the corner. Then I bolted to Kristy's house, so I could get a ride across town to the meeting.

When Kristy, Abby, and I walked into Claudia's room, Stacey and Dawn were sprawled on Claudia's bed, while Mallory and Jessi sat on the floor.

"Where's Claudia?" I asked.

"In the bathroom," Jessi answered. Kristy walked over to Claudia's computer to look at something. When I saw what it was, I couldn't help looking closely also. Claudia's playground application was on the screen.

"Look." Kristy pointed to the part of the application that asked about availability. Claudia had written that if she gets the playground job, she wouldn't go to Europe.

"That's the perfect answer," Kristy congratulated Claudia when she returned to the room.

"What?" said Claudia.

"Your answer about being available for the playground job," Kristy explained, pointing at the computer. "It's perfect because it doesn't tie you down. I mean, if you get the job, you can still ask later if you can go on the trip."

Claudia looked puzzled. "Kristy, I just wrote the truth. If I get the playground job, I'm not going to Europe."

"What?" Kristy couldn't believe it.

"Claudia!" Stacey gasped.

"I like what Claudia did. It's honest," I couldn't help putting in. "You can't say you're available for a job all summer when you're planning to leave for a week."

"Mary Anne?" Kristy turned to me with her hands on her hips. "Are *you* planning to ditch the trip if you get a playground job?"

I started to cry — just a little. I couldn't help it.

"I've decided to stay home even if I *don't* get a playground job. I want to spend more time with Dawn," I admitted.

"I thought you might feel that way," Kristy said. She glared at me. I knew she was disappointed. As for Dawn — well, she just looked thrilled. At least that made me feel better.

"This meeting will come to order," Kristy growled. I looked at the clock. It was 5:35 P.M., one of the first times in BSC history we had ever started late. This led to one of the worst meetings I can remember. It was even worse than the past meeting, and that's saying a lot. No one was hungry, not even Claudia, who listlessly unwrapped a Ring-Ding and then just stared at it.

We fielded at least ten baby-sitting calls, which was good, but we argued about who was going to take the assignments.

"I think the people going to London and Paris should get priority," Kristy insisted. "After all, we're the ones who need to raise money for plane fare and travel expenses."

"Not fair," Dawn said. "We all need money in the summer."

It turned out that Abby, Stacey, and Kristy were free most often, and they received seven out of the ten assignments. Claudia and Dawn weren't happy about this.

We did move on to Pizza Express at six o'clock as planned. But by then, Dawn and Kristy were barely speaking, and the rest of us were in bad moods.

It didn't help that we couldn't agree on what to order. We had planned on splitting an extra-large pizza to save money.

"I won't eat sausage and pepperoni," Dawn was saying.

"We know," Kristy snapped. "You can just order vegetables for your side of the pizza and let us eat our meat in peace."

"Don't forget, I'm allergic to tomatoes and cheese," Abby reminded us. "So I can't have pizza at all."

We ended up ordering separate meals.

The only time anyone cheered up was when Mallory announced that her brothers were cleaning out their rooms just for us, and that they had plenty of stuffed animals they wanted to give away. "They're even parting with Snowball, that big husky."

"That's generous," Abby remarked. "Snowball will sell. I'd buy him myself, but he'd probably make me sneeze."

That was the one time all evening that anyone laughed. It must have broken the tension a little, because we were then able to settle down and plan our fund-raiser, even though we were still mad at each other.

Here are some things we decided about the fund-raiser:

1) We were going to hold it outside, weather permitting, in Dawn's and my backyard. If it rained, we could always move it to the barn, which meant, of course, that Dawn and I would have to clean the barn to get things ready, just in case. We would also have to ask Dad's and Sharon's permission.

2) Claudia was going to make all the fliers and signs to distribute around the neighborhood.

3) We would advertise the sale in the *Stoneybrook News*, our local paper. (Kristy said she would take care of that.)

4) Abby and Kristy were going to pick up donations around town. (Charlie would probably agree to drive them.)

5) We would hold the fund-raiser the following Sunday. All of us would be there to help arrange and sell the merchandise.

"We're going to have plenty of stuffed animals to sell," Abby said with confidence.

"Yeah. And plenty of grumpy baby-sitters selling them," Dawn muttered under her breath.

CHAPTER 9

Thursday

Victoria is ANGRY, very angry, at everything and everyone. And I need to learn when to keep my mouth shut.

P.S. Miss Rutherford asked me to mention that Victoria's going-away party is next Wednesday at noon. We're all invited. Miss Rutherford says it's for an early tea. Victoria insists it's a barbecue.

"I won't. NO! YOU CAN'T MAKE ME DO THAT!"

Stacey could hear Victoria shouting before she even rang the Kents' doorbell.

"Hullo, miss. This way, please," the butler said as he opened the door and led Stacey upstairs to the playroom. Several cardboard boxes, half filled with books and toys, were scattered around the room.

"NO. AND I REPEAT, NO! I'M NOT GOING TO HELP YOU PACK WHEN I DON'T EVEN WANT TO MOVE!" Victoria shouted at Miss Rutherford, who was placing a pile of comic books in one of the boxes. "NO ONE EVER ASKS ME WHAT *I* WANT TO DO."

"Vicki? Hello," Stacey calmly interrupted.

Victoria turned around.

"Hello, Stacey. Why are you whispering?"

"Because you're shouting."

The butler actually grinned as he walked out of the room.

"Please pardon our appearance," Miss Rutherford apologized, waving her hand over the boxes. "We've been packing and packing."

Victoria, flushed from yelling, scowled at her nanny.

"Now, Victoria, it's not my fault we're moving," Miss Rutherford, highly attuned to such scowls, said.

Victoria only scowled again as she plopped herself down on the sofa, where she sat with her arms folded across her chest.

"Vicki, Mary Anne told you I was coming today, didn't she?" asked Stacey.

"Yes," Victoria muttered. "She said she was helping Dawn clean out the barn for your stuffed animal sale."

Stacey nodded. "Right."

"We certainly have plenty of stuffed animals and other toys to donate to your sale," Miss Rutherford said, gesturing to a corner of the room where a huge blue-and-white stuffed rabbit sat with an armload of smaller animals in its lap.

"Mary Anne spends more time with Dawn than she does with me," Victoria remarked. She had stopped shouting.

"Well, she hasn't seen Dawn in a long time," Stacey pointed out, even though she sensed that no explanation would appease Victoria in her current mood.

"But I'm the one moving, in case you haven't noticed," Victoria said crossly. "Mary Anne can see Dawn all summer. I'm leaving at the end of June."

"I know," Stacey replied patiently. "But Dawn *is* Mary Anne's sister."

Victoria stared at Stacey in sulky silence.

"I'll just leave you two alone," Miss Rutherford said, aiming a sympathetic look at Stacey. "I have some packing to do downstairs."

"I don't know why I even bothered to make friends in America if I only have to leave them," Victoria grumbled. "I hate all this moving. It doesn't seem fair that I have to move whenever my parents do."

"Your parents do move a lot," Stacey agreed, sitting on the sofa beside Victoria.

"And no one ever asks me where I want to live — ever." Victoria stood up and kicked over her Statue of Liberty wastebasket.

"Did you visit the Statue of Liberty recently?" Stacey asked, to change the subject.

"Miss Rutherford and I went," Victoria replied sullenly, "with Mary Anne, when Mary Anne was willing to do things with me. You know — before Dawn came."

Stacey sighed and watched the wastebasket roll around the playroom. "Vicki, why don't we go outside? It's a beautiful day, and you won't have to look at all these boxes."

"I don't want to go outside."

"What about a game? Checkers or Monopoly?" (Monopoly is one of Victoria's favorites.)

"NO! Besides, they're packed."

Stacey stood up and looked in one of the boxes that held toys and books. She pulled out an atlas. "Can you show me where you live in England?" she asked.

At that, Victoria perked up a little. She not only showed Stacey where her house was, in a small town north of London, but she told her how to get to the Tower of London, the British Museum, and London's biggest department stores.

"You absolutely have to go to Harrod's," Victoria was saying. "It's not as big as Macy's, but it has divine things. You know, the *coolest* stuff."

"I'll try to get there," said Stacey. "You know how much I love to shop."

Victoria actually grinned. "I guess the only good thing about leaving is that you're all coming to visit me next month. I can't wait to show London to Mary Anne."

Stacey looked puzzled. "But Mary Anne isn't going to London."

"What?" Victoria looked stricken, then angry. "I thought she was. Why isn't she going?"

"She, well, she wants to stay in Stoneybrook with Dawn. Dawn isn't going to London either," Stacey answered lamely. She now realized she shouldn't have said anything about Mary Anne's plans.

"NO!" Victoria screamed. "I WANT MARY ANNE TO VISIT ME!" She stamped her foot.

"But Victoria —"

"And why didn't Mary Anne tell me herself? Doesn't she care about me at all?"

"Of course she does. You mean a lot to her."

"Well, it doesn't seem as though I do." Victoria's eyes were flashing. "Now that I'm moving, she just doesn't care. She doesn't even visit. She doesn't care about anyone but Dawn."

"Victoria —" Stacey was at a loss for words.

"Well," Victoria humphed as she folded her arms across her chest, "if that's how she's going to act, I don't want her for a friend anymore. And you can tell her that."

By now, tears were streaming down Victoria's face. And she was still very, very angry when Stacey left an hour later.

CHAPTER 10

As soon as she arrived home, Stacey called me.

"Mary Anne, you won't believe what I've done," she began.

Before I could say anything, Stacey told me the story of her afternoon with Victoria. "I'm so sorry, Mary Anne. I had no idea Victoria thought you were going on the trip," she finished.

"It's not your fault. I should have told Victoria myself the last time I saw her. I guess I just didn't want to give her more bad news when she was already so upset about moving."

"I understand. It's just that Victoria is so angry right now. And telling her this news didn't help."

"I'll visit her first thing tomorrow," I said.

After Stacey and I hung up, I felt awful. I had no idea how much my going to London had meant to Victoria.

* * *

I was very nervous when I arrived at the Kents' mansion on Friday morning. Would Victoria speak to me? Would we be able to have a decent conversation? Would she forgive me?

I gulped and tried to collect myself before I rang the bell.

Miss Rutherford opened the door. "Oh, hello, Mary Anne."

"Hi. Is Victoria home?"

Miss Rutherford hesitated. "Yes, she is. But she does not wish to see you." Miss Rutherford said this very dramatically.

"Really?" I replied in a small voice. (I had been afraid of this.)

"Well, not today, certainly."

"Are Lady Kent and Sir Charles home?" I asked. (I thought that maybe if I talked to Victoria's parents about what had happened, they could explain to Victoria and then maybe she would see me.)

"Sir Charles and Lady Kent are in Brussels," Miss Rutherford answered. "Perhaps you should come back in a few days, when things have blown over. You know how sensitive Victoria is. Just give her some time."

"All right," I said. "I'll do that. But I'll probably write her a note in the meantime."

"Very well," Miss Rutherford said as she closed the front door.

*   *   *

I thought about what I would write to Victoria. First I would apologize for not telling her my plans. Then I would tell her how sorry I was that I was not going to England, but that I would make plans to visit another time. That sounded pretty good.

At home, I meant to go straight to my room to write my note to Victoria. But first, I needed a cold drink.

Then I made myself a small midmorning snack.

Then I called Logan. He thought it was a good idea to write Victoria a note. I meant to do it as soon as we hung up.

But first I washed the dishes.

Then I fed and played with Tigger.

Then I noticed the answering machine was blinking. I pressed the button marked PLAY.

"This message is for Mary Anne and Dawn," said a familiar voice, Mrs. Simon's. I turned up the volume. "I would like you two to come in for an interview next Monday afternoon," the message continued. (All right! Dawn and I had made the first cut). Mrs. Simon went on to tell us where and when to meet her.

I was so happy that I danced around the kitchen with Tigger. Before we had circled the floor twice, Dawn came home.

"Dawn, guess what? We've been called in to interview for the playground jobs."

"Both of us?"

"Yeah."

Dawn was happy, but not as happy as I had expected.

"Dawn, we *both* have interviews," I repeated. "Why aren't you excited?" (I could not believe Dawn wasn't thrilled. Usually, *I'm* the cautious, subdued one.)

"Oh, I *am* excited," Dawn answered. "It's just that, well . . ."

"What? What's wrong?"

"I'm just concerned that you really wanted to go to Europe and that you're staying in Stoneybrook all summer because of me," Dawn finally said.

"Oh, no, Dawn. I want to be home for lots of reasons. Yes, I do want the time with you. But don't forget, Logan is home all summer too. And I want to spend more time with him. You know how busy he is during the school year."

Dawn nodded. She looked as though she were feeling better but not completely convinced.

"Besides," I added, "I also promised to help Dad with the garden this summer."

"Don't mention gardening to me," Dawn said, grinning, as she held up her callused fingers. "Look what the lawn mower did to me." (Dawn insisted on using my dad's old manual lawnmower because it doesn't burn gasoline.)

We laughed. Then I told Dawn again how much I was looking forward to our being playground counselors together.

"Let's just hope we both get jobs," Dawn said. "You know how much competition there's going to be. I think it's very possible that one of us will get a job and the other one won't. We have to be ready for that."

"I know," I said. "And, I admit, the thought of only one of us getting a job does bother me. But it's not worth letting it ruin our summer. There will still be plenty of baby-sitting jobs."

"I agree," Dawn said. "Plus, our time together is too important."

"I'll say."

"I do feel better, Mary Anne. I'm glad we had this talk."

"Me too," I said. Then I told Dawn what had happened at Victoria's house.

"She really had her nanny tell you she wouldn't see you?" Dawn was aghast.

"I'm going to write her an apology note," I said.

"Why don't we go out to lunch first — to celebrate our interviews."

I thought about my note to Victoria. I decided it could wait.

"Let's go," I said, grabbing my purse.

But before we could leave, the phone rang. It was Abby, asking if we'd heard from Mrs. Simon. Abby also had an interview on Monday.

The phone rang again and again. Kristy, Stacey, and Logan had interviews too. But Mallory and Jessi had both been cut, along with all the other sixth-graders. They were *not* happy, to say the least. But they weren't taking it personally.

The last caller was Claudia. She too had an interview on Monday, but she was very worried that her academic performance would kill her chances.

"Oh, Claud, that has nothing to do with being good with kids, which is what they're looking for. They want people with a lot of baby-sitting experience, like you."

"You really think so?"

"Yes. And they probably want people who can do a lot of arts and crafts with the kids on rainy days."

"Well, that's true," said Claudia, sounding more reassured. "I can certainly do arts and crafts."

By the time I got off the phone with Claudia, Dawn had made us a delicious lunch, so we stayed at home after all.

It was midafternoon when I *finally* settled down to write to Victoria. Although I had composed the note in my head (sort of), it was not easy to write. I read each draft aloud to Dawn. It was almost dinnertime when the note was finished:

Dear Vicki:

I am very sorry I will not be coming to visit you in England this summer. I am also sorry I did not tell you this news myself, but I only decided a few days ago. And since you were so upset about moving, I did not want to give you more bad news. I hope you understand.

Maybe I will be able to visit you in England another time. Then you can show me around your house and take me to all your favorite places in London.

I have really enjoyed becoming your friend. And I will miss you very, very much when you leave.

I hope we can always keep in touch.

Your baby-sitter and friend,
Mary Anne

CHAPTER 11

I delivered Victoria's note in person and left it with the butler on Friday evening.

On Saturday, I did not hear a word from Victoria. But I was too busy to think about it much. For one thing, Dawn and I were struggling to make our yard look presentable for the BSC fund-raiser.

We mowed. We raked. We weeded. We pruned.

When Logan came over, he helped us haul our long folding tables out of the barn so we could clean them off.

By the time the other BSC members dropped off donations, there was a clean space in the barn in which to put everything, and the yard looked "wonderful" — Mallory's word. "I'll be here early to help you set up," she told me.

"Be here by eight o'clock," said Kristy, who was standing nearby unloading a huge bag of stuffed animals from her brother's car. "The sale begins at nine-thirty sharp."

Mallory's eyes flashed. "I know it begins at nine-thirty," she snapped. "Why are you always treating me like your little sister or something?"

"I'm just trying to make sure we're on top of things."

Dawn wiped sweat off her face with a pink bandanna. "I just hope it's not this hot tomorrow," she said, probably to change the subject.

"It's supposed to be," said Claudia, who was lugging art supplies and poster board to the barn. Then she added, "I have some signs and other decorations at home. The paint's drying."

"Just be here early to put them up," Kristy requested.

"Of course I will." Claudia sounded annoyed. "And why are you always bossing everyone around?"

"Someone has to organize this sale," Kristy snapped. "And I don't see *you* volunteering."

Claudia glared.

I sighed.

I wished everyone would stop being so competitive.

Kristy didn't have to worry about everyone arriving early. On Sunday morning, Claudia, Shannon, and Logan showed up at seven-thirty, ten minutes before Kristy and a half hour before the others.

Luckily we were so busy setting things up that we didn't have time to fight.

By nine o'clock, the long tables were piled high with stuffed rabbits, zebras, giraffes, monkeys, dogs, cats, koalas, lions, polar bears, and crocodiles — to name a few. We had grouped the animals by kind, so the dogs had an entire table to themselves. The tables were decorated with balloons and crepe paper. And we had put name tags on the animals whose names we knew: a bloodhound named Baskerville; a groundhog called Shadow; Demitasse, a worn gray poodle; and my favorite, Matilda the kangaroo.

I must admit, some of the animals looked pretty scruffy, but Claudia had tied bright ribbons around the necks of the most worn ones.

"The best-loved ones," Mallory insisted.

"That's one way of looking at it," Claudia muttered as she knotted a purple bow around a scraggly white rabbit named Snowball.

"You know, we have a lot of animals named Snowball," I remarked, pointing to a polar bear, the Pike triplets' husky, and now the rabbit.

"They must have all been White Christmas presents," joked Abby.

"Very funny," Claudia said as she fluffed the

hair on a panda, who did not have a name.

Besides the stuffed animals, we were selling toys and old children's books. (The books had been my idea.) I put a *Curious George* volume in the arms of Dawn's old Curious George monkey. A copy of *The Runaway Bunny* sat on the lap of Victoria's huge blue-and-white rabbit. *Babar* board books stood next to the elephants.

"I think we should give free books to the kids buying the oldest-looking animals," Abby suggested.

Kristy shook her head. "You'd be surprised at what sells," she said.

By nine-thirty, ten carloads of kids had arrived. By ten, we'd run out of food.

All morning, kids milled around the yard. Almost all of our baby-sitting charges showed up.

The Pike triplets decided they wanted their husky back. (We gave it to them for free.)

Karen Brewer, Hannie Papadakis, and Nancy Dawes bought our entire poodle collection.

Linny Papadakis and Scott Hsu fought over the tiger. (We compromised by finding a lion for Scott.)

Jenny Prezzioso insisted on buying Victoria's huge blue-and-white rabbit, despite her mother's protests that Jenny already had enough stuffed animals. (We agreed with her mother, but Jenny got her way.)

By one o'clock, we were sold out! Even the scruffiest animals were gone.

"There's no accounting for taste," Dawn said as we were cleaning up.

"Wasn't it great that all our baby-sitting charges came?" said Abby.

"All except Victoria," I remarked. (That reminded me; I was supposed to baby-sit for Victoria next Tuesday. I wondered if the job was still on.)

"We made a fortune," Stacey jubilantly proclaimed. "Almost five hundred dollars, including money from selling refreshments and donations from parents."

"With that and the other jobs we're doing, we'll all raise half our airfare," Kristy remarked.

Stacey was busy writing in her notebook. "Well, we do have to reimburse Claudia for her art supplies, and Dawn and Mary Anne for the food, and Charlie for gas money. But we still made a healthy profit."

"Don't forget, we'll be earning a lot on the playground," Abby said.

"Yeah, you will," Mallory couldn't help remarking.

"Sorry," Abby replied quickly.

"We probably won't all get playground jobs," Logan observed as he took apart the lemonade booth.

"Party pooper," said Kristy, looking annoyed.

"It's true," said Dawn. "We might as well be prepared for that."

"Well, I'm planning to get one." Kristy sounded defiant.

"What makes you so sure you will?" Claudia asked. "You're going to Europe, remember?"

"I still think I'll get the job. It's better to be positive in the interview. Besides, I have more baby-sitting and camp-counseling experience than almost all the other applicants."

"Bully for you," muttered Abby.

By three o'clock, the yard was cleaned up, but hardly any of the BSC members felt like talking to one another.

CHAPTER 12

That night I tossed and turned in bed for a long time. I could not stop thinking about the next day's interviews. The next morning, I could tell Dawn hadn't slept well either. For one thing, she was up early, earlier than I was, which is unusual. At breakfast, she was rubbing her eyes, and she did not even seem excited when Dad made us a California breakfast Dawn-style — fresh-squeezed orange juice, whole-grain wheat muffins, and fresh strawberries and peaches.

"What's with you guys?" Jeff asked as he helped himself to his third muffin.

"We're just stressed about our interviews this afternoon," Dawn said as she moved strawberries around on her plate.

"I'm sure you both stand a very good chance of getting jobs," Dad assured us. (And he is not one to make remarks like that casually.) "I think it should help that neither of you is going to Europe."

"I think so too," I said.

"Let's just hope the ones planning to go on the trip admit it," Dawn said dryly.

Dawn and I were still nervous when we walked to Stoneybrook Middle School that afternoon. The interviews began at four and would last until six. Jessi and Mal were covering the BSC meeting for us since everyone else in the club, except Shannon, would be interviewing.

I felt even more nervous when I saw how many people were in the waiting room. Besides Kristy, Stacey, Abby, Claudia, and Logan, I also found Cokie Mason, Alan Gray, Emily Bernstein, Katie Shea, Howie Johnson, Ashley Wyeth, Penny Weller, and at least ten other kids from my class. In addition, there were a whole bunch of high school kids at the other end of the room, presumably there for the senior positions.

"Look, even Janine is applying," Dawn said, touching my arm.

"Amazing," I replied. Somehow I couldn't picture Claudia's brainy sister on the playground. But why not?

"I don't see Brad Simon," I whispered to

Dawn. "He really wanted a job. But I'm not surprised he didn't make the cut. He's been suspended for cheating."

"Hi, guys," Claudia said, waving us over. "I am *so* nervous. I hope that if Janine gets a job, I get one too. Or it's going to be kind of awkward in our house."

"I know what you mean," Dawn said, giving me a Look.

This conversation was not helping my nerves. I was glad when Mrs. Simon came out to talk to us.

"Thank you all for coming," she said in a loud voice. Almost everyone stopped talking, except Alan Gray, of course, who was telling a joke to Howie.

"Your attention, please," Mrs. Simon requested, giving Alan a Look. (I personally could not believe Alan even made the first cut.) "Since we have so many good applicants, in the interest of time, we would like the interviews to go quickly."

"Thank goodness," Claudia muttered under her breath.

"Please come into the interview room as soon as your name is called," Mrs. Simon continued as she pointed in the direction of a large office off the waiting room.

Besides Mrs. Simon, three other people were

conducting interviews: Mrs. Boyden, Mr. De Young (two other SMS teachers), and a woman I didn't know.

Emily Bernstein, Grace Blume, and Logan were the first students to be called in our age group.

"They're going alphabetically," Dawn said, sighing. Kristy drummed her fingers on her knee. Abby got up and walked around the room. Claudia rustled her Hershey bar wrapper.

"I wish Ashley wasn't applying. She's a great artist, and she's got much better grades than I do," Claudia said in a loud whisper. I think she meant only for me to hear. Unfortunately, Ashley perked up at the sound of her name and looked suspiciously at Claudia. Kristy told Claudia (rather gruffly) to stop worrying about her grades.

"Easy for you to say," Claudia snapped.

"Naww," I could hear Logan's drawl behind the wall. "I'm not on any sports teams this summer. I'll have time for the kids."

Great, I thought. *Why don't they make these walls more soundproof?*

"You're full of it," Howie muttered later on when he heard Alan Gray telling his interviewer he knew CPR and had lots of baby-sitting experience.

"I'll say," Kristy agreed. She looked at Howie and shook her head.

Some of the other kids looked mad. I vowed to speak very softly when my turn came.

The interviews went quickly. Claudia spoke so softly that no one in the waiting room could hear her, though I must admit we tried. We did hear Stacey telling her interviewer that yes, she would miss a week if she went to Europe, but she could very easily find a substitute for herself. She said she hadn't even completely decided she was going.

"That's news to me," I whispered. "I thought she'd already decided for sure."

"She has," Kristy said. "She's just trying to downplay her trip."

"But that's not right," I said crossly. "She's misleading her interviewer."

Kristy gave me a dirty look.

"Miss Goody-Two-Shoes," someone in the waiting room whispered. I could feel my face turning red. Now I was embarrassed as well as mad.

Dawn and I heard Cokie Mason's interviewer saying she would make a "splendid counselor."

"Huh?" Dawn and I said together. We shook our heads in disbelief. We think Cokie is one of the most superficial people in the eighth grade. As we listened to her interview more closely, it became apparent that Cokie's interviewer was a close friend of the Masons.

"Great," Dawn muttered. "That's one less slot open."

"Not fair." I was steaming.

"We can't do anything about it," Kristy said, but she sounded upset too.

"We've just got to build ourselves up," Abby advised.

During Abby's interview, I could hear her doing just that. When Mrs. Simon asked her how she would handle a group of cantankerous kindergartners who refused to listen to instructions, Abby said she would suggest they form teams and play a game everyone agreed on. "Kids seem to forget what they're mad about when they're involved in a game," Abby said. "And I know a lot of younger kids often feel frustrated because they're too young for the sports teams at school."

"Hey, that's *my* idea," Kristy muttered to no one in particular. "I was the one who thought of the Krushers." (The Krushers is a softball team Kristy organized for very young kids.)

"I play on several varsity teams," Abby was saying. Her voice carried well into the waiting room. "I would be more than qualified to coach soccer, softball, volleyball, basketball, and badminton."

"I don't believe her. What a show-off." Kristy was clenching her fists.

"Kristy, relax," said Dawn.

"I can't. She's stealing my strategies."

Dawn rolled her eyes.

And then Mr. De Young called my name. (Why did I have to be interviewed by a gym teacher?)

I didn't think my interview went well — to say the least. Mr. De Young asked me a lot of questions about sports: "Have you ever coached a team?" "Have you played on a team at school?" "Would you be able to organize and supervise a team of little kids?"

Ugh. What could I say? I answered no to the first two questions and hesitated on the third. "I guess so," I said. "If it were a relay race or a badminton game or something." (I know I didn't sound very confident.) At the end of my interview, I did point out that there are other things to do on the playground besides playing team sports.

"What would you suggest?" asked Mr. De Young.

Luckily, I had a ready answer for that one. I'd certainly taken enough of my baby-sitting charges to the playground. "Lots of little kids like to play hide-and-seek or tag. And they like to pretend they're pirates or cops and robbers." I went on to tell Mr. De Young how I had helped kids put on plays, make up games about being playground monsters, and tell stories.

Mr. De Young listened patiently. But at the end of my interview, he told me sports were important at a summer playground camp.

Okay. I had blown it.

When I returned to the waiting room, I could tell by Dawn's face that her interview had not gone much better than mine.

Claudia also looked upset. "They asked me about being put back to seventh grade," she told me.

"Oh, Claud," I said. "It can't matter that much."

It didn't help to hear Kristy in her interview claiming ownership of the team sports idea for little kids.

"The nerve. She's not the only one who thought of that idea. I organized my charges into a soccer team when I was living on Long Island," Abby said.

Claudia shook her head. "Sometimes Kristy thinks she's the only one with any ideas."

"If I get the job, I'll think twice about going to London and Paris," Kristy assured her interviewer.

"What!" Claudia exclaimed. We couldn't believe it.

When Kristy emerged from the interview room, she was smiling. "I think it went well," she said when Stacey asked her about her interview.

Outside, Claudia asked Kristy and Stacey if they really would think twice about going to Europe.

"I just didn't want to sound too committed to the trip in the interview," Kristy replied. "I didn't say I wasn't going."

"Yeah, I didn't either," Stacey added, but she looked uncomfortable.

"But you didn't exactly say you were going either," Claudia pointed out.

"Since when are you so picky about language?" Kristy asked.

Stacey gave Claudia a dirty look.

"Kristy," I began, "Claudia was only asking why you weren't being one hundred percent honest about the trip in your interview."

"Right," said Claudia. "I was honest on my application."

Kristy stopped in her tracks and glared at all of us. "What is this, you guys? I repeat: I never said I wasn't going to London and Paris. I just downplayed the trip because I wanted them to know I am totally committed to working with kids. You know that."

"I also know that when you want something, nothing stops you," Claudia said.

"What do you mean by that?" Kristy sounded furious.

"I mean, you like to bulldoze the competition!" Now Claudia was shouting too.

"You're just jealous because I might have a better chance at this job than you think you do. I can't help it if you have no confidence."

"Claudia has confidence," I informed Kristy.

"Mary Anne, stay out of this," Kristy snapped.

"Don't talk to her like that," said Logan.

"Yeah, you're being a bully," Claudia exclaimed.

"Guys," said Dawn. But she did not look too happy with Kristy either.

I was beginning to wish the playground jobs had never existed.

CHAPTER 13

Dawn and I spent most of Monday night feeling bad about how our interviews went and how we had all fought afterward.

On Tuesday we weren't feeling much better. But I didn't have time to sit around and brood. I had to get ready for my baby-sitting job at Victoria's house.

Since I still hadn't heard from Victoria, I expected to be turned away at her door again. But I wanted to be prepared anyway. I put on a summer dress and sandals, since the Kents are pretty formal. And I added some glitter pens and magazines to my Kid-Kit. (I thought Victoria might like the pictures of New York City in the magazines.) I said good-bye to Dawn (who told me I looked very professional) and to Jeff (who told me I could make Victoria laugh with a bunch of his jokes). Then I was off.

And you know what?

I was not turned away at the door.

In fact, Miss Rutherford told me my letter had been "warmly received."

"Good," I said, breathing a sigh of relief as I followed her to the playroom.

Victoria sat on her overstuffed couch, reading *Harriet the Spy*. "Uh, hello, Mary Anne," she greeted me shyly.

"Hello, Vicki." I sat on the couch. "That was one of my favorite books when . . ." (I had started to say "when I was about your age," but I realized that sounded a little condescending.)

"I love it," Victoria interrupted. "Harriet writes such funny notes about her neighbors."

I nodded. Though I hadn't read the book recently, I still remembered the story about Harriet, who wanted to be a writer and who carried a notebook wherever she went so she could write down all her observations about the people in her Manhattan neighborhood.

"I want to be a writer when I grow up, just like Harriet," Victoria announced.

"You'll make a good one," I said, grinning.

"You really think so?"

"Yes. You're very observant and curious, and you love to read. Those are all good qualities for being a writer someday, I think."

Victoria laughed. "Oh, good," she said, putting her book aside. "Mary Anne, do you know that Miss Rutherford has the coolest afternoon planned?"

"She does?"

"Yes. You, me, Miss Rutherford, and a few of my friends are going to the mall."

"The mall?"

"Yes. Miss Rutherford says I probably want one last dose of American culture. And you know how much I love Washington Mall. It's the best."

I nodded.

Downstairs, the doorbell was ringing.

Before long, Karen Brewer, Charlotte Johanssen, Maria Kilbourne, Becca Ramsey, Victoria, Miss Rutherford, and I were seated in the Kents' limousine, while George, their American chauffeur, headed toward the mall.

"We're off to see the maw-allll, the wonderful, wonderful mall." Karen was singing to a tune from *The Wizard of Oz*, which happens to be one of Victoria's favorite movies.

"With this entertainment, I won't have to turn on the radio," George joked.

Miss Rutherford's smile seemed frozen. She was probably thinking it was going to be a *long* afternoon.

"I just love this fountain," Victoria said as she stepped out of the limo and gazed at the marble fountain in the center of the mall. It was shooting a spray of pink water high into the air.

People outside the mall stopped to watch us get out of the limo.

"Who is she?" someone asked George as Victoria stepped forward.

"Sleeping Beauty," George answered with a straight face. "She's just woken up from her hundred-year nap. Isn't that right, Vic?"

"Why don't we go inside?" Miss Rutherford suggested as the rest of us tumbled out of the limo.

Inside, Karen put her hands over Victoria's eyes and led her down one of the long hallways. "What do you smell?" she asked.

Victoria turned up her nose and sniffed the air.

"Perfume and shampoo." (We were near a beauty parlor.)

"Now what?" asked Karen as we walked on.

"Those marvelous American hot dogs, and french fries, and fried chicken, and"— another sniff —"I think I smell doughnuts."

"You do. We're near Donut Delite," Karen informed us.

"I'm hungry," Becca announced. It turned out we all were. We took Victoria to the food court, where she had a hot dog, a corn dog, and a big plate of french fries.

"Real American food," Victoria said happily as she squirted a generous glop of ketchup on her fries.

Miss Rutherford shuddered. The rest of us tried not to laugh.

"Save room for dessert," Karen said. "We can get great ice-cream sundaes at Friendly's."

"Lovely," Victoria proclaimed.

"Maybe we should take a little walk first," Maria suggested.

"Good idea," I said.

"No problem," Victoria assured us. And indeed it wasn't a problem. Victoria had a list of things she wanted to see in the mall, and she had four eager tour guides.

Miss Rutherford and I struggled to keep up as Victoria and her friends waltzed through the video store, where Victoria bought four "truly American movies": *The Wizard of Oz, Toy Story, King Kong,* and *Home Alone.* She would have bought even more had Miss Rutherford not stopped her.

"Next stop is Steven E, where you can get some American clothes," Karen announced.

Miss Rutherford sighed, but she and I watched patiently while the girls tried on leggings, leopard-print shirts, sundresses, hats, and what seemed like every pair of sunglasses in the store.

"You should definitely buy that outfit,"

Karen told Victoria as she modeled a hot pink shirt over black-and-pink-striped leggings. "Here are some pink sunglasses to go with it."

"I love it," Victoria said, putting on the sunglasses. "Are these what you call 'cool pink shades'?"

The others laughed.

"I definitely want this outfit," said Victoria, turning to see her reflection in the floor-length mirror.

"What are your parents going to think?" Miss Rutherford asked.

"They said I could buy some genuine American clothes."

"The shirt was made in China," Karen pointed out as she read the label.

"Big deal," Becca said. "It's still a cool outfit."

Victoria bought it, along with lime-green leggings, a wild green-and-black-print shirt, and a pair of orange sunglasses, just in case her pink pair got lost.

"What about this hat?" Maria asked, handing Victoria a straw boater.

Victoria waved it away. "Too British," she said.

"I guess that means we're not going to Laura Ashley," I commented.

"I don't know what her parents are going to say about those clothes," Miss Rutherford told me when the others were out of earshot. "But it's Victoria's day. I'm trying dreadfully hard not to interfere."

"They're nice clothes," I assured her.

"I don't approve of leggings on little girls. Neither will her parents."

I hid my grin.

"My shoes are killing me," Miss Rutherford complained as we walked out of yet another store half an hour later.

"Should we stop at a shoe store?" Maria inquired.

"That won't be necessary," Miss Rutherford answered.

After a tour of Bookcenter, where I bought Victoria a copy of *The Witch of Blackbird Pond*, the other girls decided they wanted to buy her little gifts too. Karen raced into a novelty store and came out with miniature Coca-Cola bottle earrings. Victoria was thrilled. "I so love Coca-Cola," she said, putting them on.

Charlotte, Becca, and Maria presented Victoria with a cowgirl hat they bought at J. C. Penney's. "You should really try on the suede outfit, holster, and boots that go with the hat," Becca suggested.

Victoria looked interested, but Miss Rutherford said she thought Victoria had tried on quite enough clothes for the day.

"Let's have those ice-cream sundaes, shall we?" Victoria suggested as she raced her friends to Friendly's. We sat in a booth and ordered banana splits.

"With lots of chocolate sauce and marshmallows, please," Victoria told the waitress. "And those sugary-tasting cherries on top."

When the ice cream came, Victoria made quick work of hers. And on the way out of the mall, she insisted we stop at Donut Delite so she could buy one of her favorite American foods: jelly doughnuts.

I must say, I was happy to sink into the soft leather seats of the limo. Miss Rutherford seemed relieved too. We dropped Victoria's friends off first. Then, as we were on the way to my house, Victoria turned to me, her face smeared with sugar from her jelly doughnut.

"You know, Mary Anne, this has been an absolutely perfect day. I'm so happy all my friends could come with me to the mall like this, including you."

I was glad Victoria said that, because it meant she wasn't mad at me anymore.

"I was delighted to come along," I told her.

Victoria licked jelly off her fingers and grinned at me.

I was going to be sorry to see her go.

"Don't forget about the party tomorrow," Victoria reminded me as we pulled up to my house.

"I won't," I assured her.

I wouldn't miss it for the world.

CHAPTER 14

Wednesday

All I can say is, the British sure know how to throw a great party. It's too bad some of us (and I won't mention any names, Kristy) were too angry to enjoy it.

I don't know about you guys, but I can't wait to visit the Kents in England.

Ta-ta.

P.S. Talk to Vicki if you want to learn more British expressions.

"Whoa, potato chips in sterling silver bowls," Abby said to Mal as they entered the Kent mansion for Victoria's going-away party. They were among the first BSC members to arrive. In the entryway, small silver bowls held salted nuts and potato chips, and balloons were tied to the chairs.

"It sure looks festive in here," Mal remarked.

"Oh, Abigail, how lovely to see you," said Lady Kent, sweeping into the room.

"Charmed," Sir Charles added, shaking Abby's hand.

"Victoria is entertaining her friends on the sunporch," Lady Kent informed them.

"She insisted on having a barbecue," Sir Charles said. "Such a whimsical idea."

"But I believe for a true barbecue, you need a grill of some sort, don't you?" Lady Kent asked.

"You need a barbecue," Mal said helpfully.

"Right," said Lady Kent, sounding a bit distracted. "Well, we don't have one, so the cook agreed to roast everything in the kitchen. You know, the chicken, hamburgers, and so forth."

"That sounds great," Abby said, hiding her smile.

On the sunporch, the party was just beginning. Karen, David Michael, and Kristy were already there, and plenty of other people were expected, including the rest of the BSC members.

Karen and David Michael greeted Abby and Mal warmly, but Kristy barely said hello.

She was obviously still mad about the playground interviews and the fight afterward.

Luckily no one seemed to notice Kristy's cool welcome. Miss Rutherford was busy supervising the cook and butler as they set up platters of food on the sunporch and in the rose garden outside. "We're expecting a lot of people, so I am sure the party will spill over to the garden," Miss Rutherford explained.

Abby eyed the serving dishes. There were platters of little tea sandwiches, cookies, scones, and little cakes.

"The real barbecue food will be coming," Victoria promised.

"I think this looks great," Karen said, helping herself to a scone. "What are these?"

"Scones," Victoria explained, sighing. "They're heavy pastries the British have with their tea."

"I like it," Karen said, in between bites.

"And I love *this*," David Michael added, swallowing a bite-size chocolate raspberry cake.

"Where is all the American food?" Victoria wanted to know.

"Coming, miss," the butler answered. "We're waiting until more guests arrive before we bring out the hot things."

"Oh, this is going to be the most marvelous — I mean, the *greatest* — party," Victoria said, clapping her hands together. "A magician is coming, and we have all sorts of games planned."

Abby noticed that Victoria was wearing one of her new outfits — the pink shirt with the black-and-pink leggings. And her parents didn't seem to mind.

Half an hour later, the party was in full swing. Many of our baby-sitting charges were there, including Hannie and Linny Papadakis; Bill and Melody Korman; Charlotte Johanssen; Becca Ramsey, who arrived with Jessi; and Tiffany and Maria Kilbourne, who arrived with Shannon.

Abby noticed that Kristy was being friendly to Jessi and Shannon, but she hardly said a word to Dawn and me when we arrived. Abby sighed and hoped the other BSC members would not act the same way.

No such luck.

Claudia and Stacey arrived together, but they both looked grumpy, as if they had just been fighting. Claudia and Kristy refused to talk to each other, which made Abby even less eager to talk to Kristy. And Dawn, who had been acting pretty cool, decided that if that was the way her friends were going to behave, she would not have anything to do with them — not at this party, anyway. Ugh.

Shannon and Logan were the only ones acting decent. So were Jessi and Mallory, even though they were still upset about not being interviewed. Unlike some people, they knew enough not to let their feelings get in the way of a great party.

And it *was* a great party. Abby told me she loved the Kents' version of a barbecue. The butler and one of the cooks served us hamburgers on silver platters.

"What about the buns?" Victoria wanted to know.

"Pardon?" asked the butler.

Dawn put her hand in front of her face to keep from laughing out loud.

"We're bringing out some toast for the hamburgers in a minute," said Miss Rutherford.

"Toast?" David Michael stared at the hamburger on his plate.

"What about English muffins?" Linny asked.

"There's nothing English about English muffins," Miss Rutherford informed him with a slight sniff. "Forks and other utensils are over

118

there." Miss Rutherford pointed to a long table on one side of the large porch.

The table also held pots of relish, mustard, and ketchup, and bowls of potato salad, green salad, potato chips, and pretzels. Sparkling crystal glasses and iced pitchers of lemonade and Coca-Cola were on another table, along with paper cups and napkins for the younger kids.

"Are you sure this is Coca-Cola?" Mallory eyed the pitcher suspiciously.

"Positive," Abby answered. "I just asked Miss Rutherford."

"Sugar for your lemonade, miss?" asked the butler as he placed a bowl filled with sugar cubes and a pair of silver tongs next to her.

"Uh, yes," Abby said. When the butler just stood there, she decided he was waiting for her to serve herself. It took her awhile to get used to the tongs, but she managed it.

"Well done," the butler complimented her.

Abby looked around, worried that some of the kids would break their glasses or spill their drinks, but the Kents did not seem to be bothered by this. Everyone was on their best behavior. Except the BSC members.

Kristy refused to take the plate of chicken Miss Rutherford asked me to hand her.

Claudia would not answer when Abby asked her where the bathroom was.

Stacey told Claudia she was acting like a baby in front of Karen, Hannie, and David Michael, who all thought that was so funny that they called Claudia a baby during the rest of the party.

The low point came when the servers brought out dessert: chocolate fudge cake, lemon tarts, and several flavors of ice cream. Miss Rutherford asked Kristy, Claudia, Dawn, and Abby to help serve the little kids their ice cream. Kristy and Claudia grabbed the ice cream scoops, and Dawn and Abby stood next to them, handing out bowls of ice cream. No one seemed to notice that we weren't getting along until Charlotte and Karen both asked for strawberry ice cream. Claudia rested her scoop on top of the carton, ready to fill their order, when Kristy snatched the carton away.

"You're too slow," she complained to Claudia. "All the ice cream will have melted by the time you get around to scooping it out."

Claudia threw the scoop on the table. "Kristy, you are way out of line," she said loudly.

Miss Rutherford stared at Kristy and Claudia, dumbfounded. Charlotte and Karen looked shocked, their eyes like saucers. Luckily, Victoria and most of the other kids were outside, watching the magic act. But the few kids in line for ice cream did not know what to say or do.

"I'm very sorry," Kristy said to Miss Rutherford. "I get impatient sometimes."

"I'm sorry too," Claudia said to the kids in line. "I didn't mean to lose my temper."

After that unpleasant episode, the club members cooled off and there were no more scenes.

I had never seen Victoria's parents so relaxed. They talked to all the guests, and they gave Abby and Kristy their address in England and directions for getting to their home. Abby and Victoria especially had seemed to bond during the party.

"We're delighted you'll be able to visit Victoria," Lady Kent said to Abby. "She is so looking forward to it."

"We are too," said Abby after she swallowed the last bite of a bite-size sandwich. "Great food," she added.

The Kents smiled. "We tried to have real American food at this party. Victoria insisted," said Sir Charles.

When the guests began to leave, Dawn asked to use the Kents' phone. "I'm going to check the message tape at home," she told Abby and me. "I'm waiting for the Wilders to call me back about a baby-sitting job tonight."

We nodded. We were busy talking to Karen and Victoria about their new pirate game.

I was eating a cucumber sandwich when Dawn returned, very excited. "Mrs. Simon called," she reported. "The counselors have been chosen!"

CHAPTER 15

"We need to talk," Kristy said from her director's chair after she had called the BSC meeting to order.

"We do," Claudia agreed. She waved a bag of tortilla chips in the air. But no one was hungry. We had all eaten plenty at Victoria's party earlier that afternoon.

By now, we knew who had been chosen to be counselors.

Dawn, Claudia, Logan, and I had gotten jobs. (I was so relieved.) Stacey, Kristy, and Abby were rejected, but since they had said on their applications that they were going on the trip to Europe, we were pretty sure that must have been a deciding factor. Which just goes to show that Kristy and Stacey weren't fooling anybody when they downplayed the trip during the interviews.

Mrs. Simon had called each of us. And she had told Kristy, Stacey, and Abby that if they had not been going to Europe, it would have been much harder to decide who to pick as counselors.

Naturally, Kristy, Abby, and Stacey were not too thrilled. They had really wanted to be counselors. But they had had good talks with Mrs. Simon. And they were beginning to see that it would have been hard for the camp to lose half their counselors for a week.

"First of all, I want to apologize for some of the things I said to Claudia and Mary Anne," Kristy continued. "I didn't mean to lose my temper like that after the interviews, but I couldn't understand why you guys were harping on the trip so much. Now that I've thought about it, I see how you felt." Kristy turned her visor around on her head. "After all, you both decided not to go if you got the jobs. And I, well, I guess I wanted it both ways."

"Me too," said Stacey.

"That's okay," said Claudia. "But did you really mean what you said about me having no confidence?"

Kristy shook her head. "I think you sometimes don't have a lot of confidence when it comes to schoolwork. But you're pretty confident about most other things."

"As you should be," Stacey added, pointing

to a gorgeous watercolor Claudia had painted of Victoria's rose garden.

"Oh, that," said Claudia. "I'm planning to give it to Vicki as a going-away present — a reminder of her home in the States."

"Do you forgive me, Mary Anne?" Kristy asked. "I didn't mean to snap at you. I know you were only coming to Claudia's defense."

"I do," I said solemnly.

"Guys, you're so formal," Mallory said.

"I apologize to you guys too," Kristy went on, turning to Jessi and Mal, who were on the floor, leaning against Claudia's bed. "I didn't mean to be so short with you."

"It's okay," said Mallory, shrugging. "I know you've been under a lot of pressure."

"Yeah," Jessi agreed. "But you didn't really think we were too young to be counselors, did you?"

"No, I didn't," Kristy assured them.

"I'm sorry I called you a bully, Kristy," Claudia said.

"Well, I admit, I can be pretty opinionated sometimes," Kristy replied.

Stacey apologized to Claudia for calling her a baby. Claudia apologized for acting like one. "I was just so tense about the interview," she explained.

"We all were," Stacey pointed out.

"I'll say," Kristy added. "You know, we shouldn't let something small like this get in the way of our club — or our friendships — ever again."

"Agreed," Dawn said.

"Should we vote on this?" Mallory joked.

We laughed. After all, we had a lot to be happy about. Great summer jobs. A great summer trip. And our great summer was just beginning!

Dear Reader,

In *Mary Anne and the Playground Fight*, the members of the Baby-sitters Club find themselves in an unusual situation. While they're good about sharing the jobs they get at club meetings, they're now fiercely competing for a limited number of jobs that they all want badly. Competition can be difficult, especially when friends are competing against one another. You may find yourself competing against a friend in sports, in school, in contests, or, like the members of the BSC, for a job. An important thing to remember when you're competing against a friend is that both your friendship and the competition are important, so it's your responsibility to do your best, honestly. You're not being fair to your friend if you don't do your best in order to let her win. And you're not being fair to *anyone* if, like Kristy, you don't play by the rules. Try keeping things out in the open. If you and a friend are competing against each other, talk about it. Tell each other what you're afraid of, and what you hope for. Then go for it. Mary Anne and her friends might have had an easier time if they had been honest with themselves and with one another from the beginning.

Happy reading,

Ann M. Martin

L. GODWIN

Ann M. Martin

About the Author

ANN MATTHEWS MARTIN was born on August 12, 1955. She grew up in Princeton, NJ, with her parents and her younger sister, Jane.

Although Ann used to be a teacher and then an editor of children's books, she's now a full-time writer. She gets ideas for her books from many different places. Some are based on personal experiences. Others are based on childhood memories and feelings. Many are written about contemporary problems or events.

All of Ann's characters, even the members of the Baby-sitters Club, are made up. (So is Stoneybrook.) But many of her characters are based on real people. Sometimes Ann names her characters after people she knows, other times she chooses names she likes.

In addition to the Baby-sitters Club books, Ann Martin has written many other books for children. Her favorite is *Ten Kids, No Pets* because she loves big families and she loves animals. Her favorite Baby-sitters Club book is *Kristy's Big Day*. (By the way, Kristy is her favorite baby-sitter!)

Ann M. Martin now lives in New York with her cats, Gussie, Woody, and Willy. Her hobbies are reading, sewing, and needlework — especially making clothes for children.

Notebook Pages

This Baby-sitters Club book belongs to ———————.

I am ——— years old and in the ——————— grade.

The name of my school is ———————————.

I got this BSC book from ———————————.

I started reading it on ——————————— and finished reading it on ———————————.

The place where I read most of this book is ———————.

My favorite part was when ———————————.

If I could change anything in the story, it might be the part when

———————————————————————.

My favorite character in the Baby-sitters Club is ———————.

The BSC member I am most like is ———————

because ———————————————————.

If I could write a Baby-sitters Club book it would be about ———

———————————————————————.

#120 Mary Anne and the Playground Fight

In *Mary Anne and the Playground Fight*, Mary Anne faces a hard choice. She has to decide whether to stay in Stoneybrook with Dawn for the summer or go on a trip to Europe with some of her friends. If I were Mary Anne, I would have chosen to _____ _____ because _____ _____. Things get rough for Mary Anne and the other members of the Baby-sitters Club when they compete for jobs at the playground camp. I had to compete with my friend once when _____ _____. What happened was _____ _____. One friend I'm always competing with is _____. One friend with whom I never compete is _____. The adults at the playground camp have a hard time choosing counselors. If I had to choose four BSC members to be playground counselors, I would choose _____,_____, _____, and _____.

MARY ANNE'S

Party girl -- age 4

Sitting for the Pikes is always an adventure.

Sitting for Andrea and Jenny Prezzioso -- a quiet moment.

SCRAPBOOK

*Logan and me.
Summer luv at Sea City.*

*My family--
Jeff, Dad and Sharon.
Dawn and me and Tigger.*

Illustrations by Angelo Tillery

Read all the books
about **Mary Anne**
in the Baby-sitters Club series
by Ann M. Martin

Look for #121

ABBY IN WONDERLAND

Grandpa Morris came in from the outdoors. The smear of dirt on his T-shirt and the trowel in his hand told me he'd been gardening. "Elsie," he said to Gram. "I was looking at the dining area of Wonderland, to the left of the throne. I'm wondering if it's going to be hard for people to maneuver around that column when they try to reach the buffet table."

Gram set her letter down on the coffee table beside me. "You might have a point," she agreed, standing up from her chair. "Let's go take a look."

She went out again with Grandpa, but I didn't follow. Instead, I sat awhile longer, thinking about the conversation we'd just had.

Gram had said she wanted to see everyone again just because she was getting old and the family was her responsibility, but I didn't buy it. She wasn't *that* old. Truthfully, she had a lot more years to catch up with everyone.

No, I felt sure there was another reason. She wanted to see everyone this summer because she had a specific reason for thinking that she might not have another summer. As much as I didn't want to believe that, it was the only conclusion I could come to.

My gaze drifted down to the letter beside me. *My Dearest Elsie*, it began. *Your parties are always such an event and it's marvelous to see the family, but this year I regret that business calls me away to . . .*

I put the letter down. Before this vacation I'd had no idea I was such a terrible snoop. But here I was, reading a piece of personal mail addressed to somebody else. It wasn't like me, I swear! It was just that not knowing if Gram was all right was making me do desperate things.

Then it hit me. There was something very definite I could do for Gram.

Collect 'em all!

100 (and more) Reasons to Stay Friends Forever!

More titles... ▸

The Baby-sitters Club titles continued...

❑ MG22880-3	#96	Abby's Lucky Thirteen		$3.99
❑ MG22881-1	#97	Claudia and the World's Cutest Baby		$3.99
❑ MG22882-X	#98	Dawn and Too Many Sitters		$3.99
❑ MG69205-4	#99	Stacey's Broken Heart		$3.99
❑ MG69206-2	#100	Kristy's Worst Idea		$3.99
❑ MG69207-0	#101	Claudia Kishi, Middle School Dropout		$3.99
❑ MG69208-9	#102	Mary Anne and the Little Princess		$3.99
❑ MG69209-7	#103	Happy Holidays, Jessi		$3.99
❑ MG69210-0	#104	Abby's Twin		$3.99
❑ MG69211-9	#105	Stacey the Math Whiz		$3.99
❑ MG69212-7	#106	Claudia, Queen of the Seventh Grade		$3.99
❑ MG69213-5	#107	Mind Your Own Business, Kristy!		$3.99
❑ MG69214-3	#108	Don't Give Up, Mallory		$3.99
❑ MG69215-1	#109	Mary Anne to the Rescue		$3.99
❑ MG05988-2	#110	Abby the Bad Sport		$3.99
❑ MG05989-0	#111	Stacey's Secret Friend		$3.99
❑ MG05990-4	#112	Kristy and the Sister War		$3.99
❑ MG05911-2	#113	Claudia Makes Up Her Mind		$3.99
❑ MG05911-2	#114	The Secret Life of Mary Anne Spier		$3.99
❑ MG05993-9	#115	Jessi's Big Break		$3.99
❑ MG05994-7	#116	Abby and the Worst Kid Ever		$3.99
❑ MG05995-5	#117	Claudia and the Terrible Truth		$3.99
❑ MG05996-3	#118	Kristy Thomas, Dog Trainer		$3.99
❑ MG45575-3		Logan's Story Special Edition Readers' Request		$3.25
❑ MG47118-X		Logan Bruno, Boy Baby-sitter		
		Special Edition Readers' Request		$3.50
❑ MG47756-0		Shannon's Story Special Edition Reader's Request		$3.50
❑ MG47686-6		The Baby-sitters Club Guide to Baby-sitting		$3.25
❑ MG47314-X		The Baby-sitters Club Trivia and Puzzle Fun Book		$2.50
❑ MG48400-1		BSC Portrait Collection: Claudia's Book		$3.50
❑ MG22864-1		BSC Portrait Collection: Dawn's Book		$3.50
❑ MG69181-3		BSC Portrait Collection: Kristy's Book		$3.99
❑ MG22865-X		BSC Portrait Collection: Mary Anne's Book		$3.99
❑ MG48399-4		BSC Portrait Collection: Stacey's Book		$3.50
❑ MG69182-1		BSC Portrait Collection: Abby's Book		$3.99
❑ MG92713-2		The Complete Guide to The Baby-sitters Club		$4.95
❑ MG47151-1		The Baby-sitters Club Chain Letter		$14.95
❑ MG48295-5		The Baby-sitters Club Secret Santa		$14.95
❑ MG45074-3		The Baby-sitters Club Notebook		$2.50
❑ MG44783-1		The Baby-sitters Club Postcard Book		$4.95

Available wherever you buy books...or use this order form.